GOOD TO BE BAD

LILI VALENTE
LAUREN BLAKELY

LAUREN & LILI BOOKS

The Gift Series

The Engagement Gift

The Virgin Gift

The Decadent Gift

The Extravagant Duet

One Night Only

One Exquisite Touch

MM Standalone Novels

A Guy Walks Into My Bar

One Time Only

The Heartbreakers Series

Once Upon a Real Good Time

Once Upon a Sure Thing

Once Upon a Wild Fling

Boyfriend Material

Special Delivery

Asking For a Friend

Sex and Other Shiny Objects

One Night Stand-In

Lucky In Love Series

Best Laid Plans

The Feel Good Factor

Nobody Does It Better

The Happy Cat Series

(co-written with Pippa Grant)

Hosed

Hammered

Hitched

Humbugged

Click here to learn more

Unzipped

Always Satisfied Series

Satisfaction Guaranteed

Instant Gratification

Overnight Service

Never Have I Ever

PS It's Always Been You

The Sexy Suit Series

Lucky Suit

Birthday Suit

From Paris With Love

Wanderlust

Part-Time Lover

One Love Series

The Sexy One

The Only One

The Hot One

The Knocked Up Plan

Come As You Are

Sports Romance

Most Valuable Playboy

Most Likely to Score

Standalones

Stud Finder

The V Card

The Real Deal

Unbreak My Heart

The Break-Up Album

21 Stolen Kisses

Out of Bounds

My One Week Husband

The Caught Up in Love Series

The Pretending Plot (previously called *Pretending He's Mine*)

The Dating Proposal

The Second Chance Plan (previously called *Caught Up In Us*)

The Private Rehearsal (previously called *Playing With Her Heart*)

Seductive Nights Series

Night After Night

After This Night

One More Night

A Wildly Seductive Night

ALSO BY LILI VALENTE

Hot Royal Romance

The Playboy Prince

The Grumpy Prince

The Bossy Prince

Learn more here

Laugh-out-Loud Rocker Rom Coms

The Bangover

Bang Theory

Banging The Enemy

The Rock Star's Baby Bargain

Learn more here

The Bliss River Small Town Series

Falling for the Fling

Falling for the Ex

Falling for the Bad Boy

Learn more here

The Hunter Brothers

The Baby Maker

The Troublemaker

The Heartbreaker

The Panty Melter

Click here to learn more

The Bad Motherpuckers Series

Hot as Puck

Sexy Motherpucker

Puck-Aholic

Puck me Baby

Pucked Up Love

Puck Buddies

Click here to learn more

Sexy Flirty Dirty Romantic Comedies

Magnificent Bastard

Spectacular Rascal

Incredible You

Meant for You

Click here to learn more

To the Bone Series

(Sexy Romantic Suspense, must be read in order)

A Love so Dangerous

A Love so Deadly

A Love so Deep

Click here to learn more

The Rebel Hearts Series

(Emotional New Adult Romantic Suspense.

Must be read in order.)

ABOUT

It was only supposed to be one time.

But that red-hot one night stand from the party?

The sexy man in the suit who gave me more Os in a few hours than I've had in a year?

Turns out my charming British stranger is keeping a little secret.

He's as much of a whiz in the kitchen as he is in the bedroom and soon we'll be going head-to-head in NYC's biggest bake off.

My one-time lover is now my enemy. I vow to loathe him for all eternity, though that would be easier if I wasn't dying to get naked with him again.

But the more I learn more about my rival, the more I suspect he just might be everything I've wanted...

If only I knew how to let him in...

GOOD TO BE BAD is a sexy standalone romance in the Good Love series!

GOOD TO BE BAD

By Lauren Blakely and Lili Valente

Want to be the first to learn of sales, new releases, preorders and special freebies? Sign up for Lauren's VIP mailing list here!

**Join Lili Valente's mailing list for all the latest news, sales, and exclusive subscriber goodies!
Subscribe here!**

HER PROLOGUE

Gigi

Some things in life need to be *just so*.

Like the pockets in the adorable A-line dress I'm wearing to a party this weekend.

The imperious expression on Gram's Maine Coon rescue cat, as she lounges on an armchair, looking like the royalty she is.

The detail in the fabulous enamel apple pie charm necklace I snagged from a retro shop in Williamsburg.

Then, there are the new menus for my shop.

My shop.

Aunt Barb and Uncle Pete retired last month and, much to my surprise, let me buy them out for five grand and a promise to keep my cousin Ruby on as my graphic designer for as long as she's interested and able. As if I would hire anyone else. Ruby isn't just my cousin, she's my best friend. And this shop...

Well, Sweetie Pies is my darling. It's already a successful business, but I intend to make it an even more delightful and delicious place to spend an afternoon. Soon, this won't just be a place to grab a slice, it will be a destination for every visitor to Greenpoint, Brooklyn.

I've spent months perfecting my renovation plans, including epic glass cases to showcase the hell out of the daily pie selection. I want those golden beauties to look so damned yummy customers will lean in and lick the glass.

But a good pie should be that seductive. It should be a crumbly, buttery, sugary fantasia that charms the tongue and enchants the senses, so when you slip the last bite between your lips, you're already planning your next trip to Sweetie Pies to experience the magic all over again.

But magic doesn't come for free.

It requires dedication, hard work, and an obsession with getting every detail *just right*. I have those things in spades, in all the important things in my life.

But Dating?

Dating didn't get the magical memo.

Dating doesn't understand it ought to be delightful, or at least not an exercise in torture.

Which is not cool, Dating. I've put in the time, my friend. I've rolled up my blouse sleeves and written clever dating profiles, planned festive get-to-know-you meet-ups, and amiably agreed to every blind date and awkward dinner party arranged by friends and family.

And yet dating remains recalcitrant.

It's a cat with a bad attitude, pretending it can't hear me begging it to play nice as it knocks over that cup of Ethiopian coffee onto my fluffy white rug with a swish of its tail.

Why can't dating be more like a Pinterest board? Beautifully curated and chock full of charming men with big, squishy hearts and massive cocks?

Instead, it's a Ouija board conjuring potential mates from the demon realm.

Like the guy who narrated our date in a whispery voice like a nature documentary—*watch the modern man in his natural habitat as he attempts to split the check without the aid of his cell phone calculator.* Or the man who said he too, loved historical romances, then brought along a friend to serve as our chaperone so my reputation wouldn't be sullied by dining alone with a member of the opposite sex.

I gave him points for creativity—cosplay can be cute —but deducted them all when the "chaperone" helped himself to my crème brûlée while I was in the ladies' room.

As a thirty-year-old single woman in New York, I'll abide some shenanigans in the name of finding true love, but I draw the line at dessert thievery.

Still, those encounters left me with funny stories to tell, and were downright marvelous compared to my long-term relationships.

Boyfriends live to break my heart. Three times has not proved the charm for this girl. I've had three steady guys, and all three suffered from chronic cases of My Peen Leaps into Other Women's Vaginas.

But I don't need true love—or a man—to be happy.

Positive Thinking is my middle name. Chin up and with my favorite berry red lipstick on, I'm living my best life all by myself.

Running my new business.

Playing sudoku with Gram.

And working on my Sweetie Pies renovation plans.

Admittedly, I wouldn't mind a little affection. A snuggle here or there. A sweet nothing whispered in my ear.

Fine, I wouldn't mind an orgasm—or ten—either. Preferably delivered by someone like Henry Cavill, Ryan Reynolds, or that guy from Bridgerton.

But will it happen?

Magic Eight Ball says...not likely. Not in this city and not with a job that requires me to be in bed by nine, far before most single men are out on the prowl. And honestly, I don't have time for another disappointing boyfriend. It's a busy life, becoming the sweet queen of Brooklyn.

So, pie is the plan, and that suits me just fine.

Until the night I hear the delicious, toe-tingling, knee weakening voice of my dream man.

What's the harm in giving in for just one night?

HIS PROLOGUE

West

Timing, as they say, is everything.

Money, for instance—you have to know when to buy and when to sell in order to reap financial rewards.

Check. Been there, done that. Have the coin to prove it.

Scones are the same—let them bake too long and you'll turn your mum's fantastic family recipe into charcoal briquettes; too soon and you've got a soggy pile of dough.

This too, is in the bag. Scones are my jam...though I prefer them with clotted cream.

Then, there's sex.

Timing is everything in the bedroom. A man needs to know precisely the right moment to kiss a woman's neck and drive her wild, to glide his hand along her waist so she shivers, to tease her with his lips until she's begging for a kiss. He needs to know when to undress her slowly and seductively, and when the night calls for ripping panties and tearing at shirts.

Timing is learning to listen to her needs, her wants, her wishes, so he can make her writhe with pleasure so sweet it's almost painful. And don't even get me started on orgasms. Those precious, life-bestowing detonations of pleasure require the precision of an atomic clock.

You have to know exactly when to thrust harder and deeper. When to grind and when to glide. When to lick, touch, and stroke.

You only get out of something what you put into it, so when it comes to making sure my lover's satisfied, I leave it all on the field. I'm a gentleman, at least in that regard, and a gentleman always makes sure a lady comes first.

And hard.

And often.

But timing isn't only paramount in the bedroom, it's critical with professional choices, as well. You must take the proper steps at the proper time to ensure success.

And success *will* be mine. Again. But this time, on my terms.

I stayed the course when I was younger. When I graduated from university, I did what was expected, plugging away in the family business. But when I hit my goals, it was time to pivot.

And pivot I did, from London to New York City.

It might seem a huge risk to up and move across the pond, but I've been prepping for years. Everything is in place, and now the stars have aligned and the timing is right. I'm in New York, ready to execute my precisely laid plans.

And then a gorgeous, brilliant, Rubik's-Cube-wielding redhead sashays into my life. There's no other way to describe the way this woman moves—like life's a dance and she's relishing every minute of it.

Too bad it turns out she's the last woman I should be dancing—or anything else—with.

Timing is everything. And this timing is about to go tits up.

1

GIGI

The new cases were installed today, and they look *amazing*.

The pie specials are prepped for tomorrow and Calliope is coming in early to start the ovens so I can sleep in.

The money is counted, the shop is spotless, and all is right with the world.

I pat the counter and blow a kiss to Sweetie Pies as I go. "Love you, darling," I say, dragging down the metal gate in front of the door and locking up for the night.

As I head down the sidewalk, I remind myself of all the good things in life. It's a nightly ritual I've done since I was a little girl.

I have my friends. My brother, Harrison. My gram. And the most fantastic business and customers in the entire world.

And it's party time!

I can't remember the last time I went to a party. Or the last time I stayed out past ten o'clock. Much like a

real offspring, my bakery baby requires certain sacri-
fices. I'm out of bed at five most mornings and up to my
elbows in dough by five fifteen. I moved to an apartment a two-minute walk from Sweetie Pies in order to
be closer to my darling girl. I love being able to stick my
head out my kitchen window and see her sitting safely
there on the corner, looking adorable and delicious.

Ruby teases me about being a helicopter pie shop
parent, but I just feel better when the things and people
I love are close.

If I had my way, Harrison and Gram would move
into the apartment above mine and Ruby and her true
love, Jesse, would move into the empty building across
the street from Sweetie Pies.

Or they *could have* moved in a month ago if some
wretched tea-peddling human hadn't snatched it up.

Ugh. Tea. It's like drinking grass juice with lemon
on top.

I hate it. And I *really* hate people who intend to sell
tea and sweet treats right across the street from my pie
shop.

I fold my arms, shivering as I pass the building in
question, looking menacing and ominous with its "Tea
and Empathy Opening Soon" sign taped in the front
window.

Why? Why must competition move in right across
the street at the exact moment I'm primed to achieve
total dessert domination of Greenpoint and greater
Brooklyn at large?

Deep breath. Everything will be fine.

The tea peddler will probably be a horrible baker

who does a piddling little business that won't interfere with mine. But as I start up the steps to my apartment, I do wish things were different.

If Ruby and Jesse had bought the place, we could have had coffee and slices together at two twenty-five each afternoon—two twenty-five being the perfect time for an afternoon treat. It's not too close to lunch and still leaves time to work up an appetite for a healthy dinner.

Or a handful of spinach eaten straight from the bag and an only slightly expired cheese wheel you dig out from behind the butter sticks in the fridge, if, say, you haven't had time to go shopping for yourself in ages.

As I bustle around my apartment, munching soggy spinach while running a bath and laying out my party dress, I promise I'll do that on my day off tomorrow. Grocery shopping isn't nearly as much fun as getting one's nails done or popping into a favorite consignment shop to try on crinolines, but it's a necessity.

And I do like to eat things other than pie.

Occasionally.

As a reward for consuming rabbit food, I pour myself a glass of pink bubbly to enjoy during my bath and settle in for a soak with a happy sigh.

The hot water feels heavenly on my aching, dough-rolling-taxed shoulders, and the champagne is sweet and fizzy on my tongue.

Yes, the world is still full of sensual delights that have nothing to do with breath-stealing kisses, ripping a man's shirt off in the heat of passion, or having him turn you over his knee for a spanking.

Mmm. Spankings. Swats. Hair pulling.

I hum under my breath to the tune of the *Sound of Music* since these are, indeed, a few of my favorite things.

Then I do my best *not* to linger on spankings because I really do love a fun, flirty spanking and it's been so very long since I enjoyed one.

Months, I think.

Many months.

Maybe close to a year?

"No. Stop. Don't," I mutter aloud.

I will *not* think of Theodore or how much fun it was to play sex games with him or how often I've run into him since we broke up without him even noticing that I'm in his general vicinity. I wear brightly colored dresses with huge fluffy skirts and, more often than not, a considerable amount of cleavage on display. Nice cleavage too, if I do say so myself.

But I am apparently invisible to the last man who gave me orgasms.

"Which is fine, because you can give yourself orgasms," I say, as my red toes peek out of my bubble bath. "Better, faster ones."

But the words don't tempt me to slide my fingers under the bubbles and between my legs the way I would have earlier in my adventure in celibacy. These days, my best bet is to not think about sex too much, even when I'm alone. It's just too frustrating. The last prospect broke up with me via parrot before we could get to orgasm territory, and I don't see an end to that frustration anywhere in sight.

Yes…a parrot.

The bird squawked, "It's *me* not you. *Me* not you. Let's break up," on cue. Did he train it to say that or did the parrot learn it since he said it so much?

Either way, dodged a bullet with that one. Besides, I'm looking forward to flying solo to this party tonight. It's so much easier to dominate at Rubik's Cube, giant Jenga, and other assorted classic games without a guy around judging my nerdish tendencies.

Maybe someday I'll meet a man who enjoys being nerdy together.

Ha. Maybe I'll ride a unicorn to the party too.

* * *

Forty minutes later, I'm breezing out of the subway into the cool night air in front of The Library, one of Brooklyn's hottest live music venues. It features a stage and dance floor surrounded by floor-to-ceiling bookshelves, including a historical romance section with a take-a-book-leave-a-book policy—be still my bookish heart.

But tonight, the floor isn't filled with thrashing punks or swaying hipsters in jeans too tight for real dancing. Instead, gamers surround tables spread with Scrabble, Clue, or Monopoly, a giant Jenga game dominates the stage, and—most tantalizing of all—the Rubik's Cube twist off tournament begins at nine. It looks like most people are competing in teams of two or three, but I'd rather go solo than risk being paired with a novice who will bring down my time.

I'm not just nerdy, I'm competitive about it.

I sign up for the second heat, wiggle my fingers for good luck at the line of cubes on the edge of the stage, and head for the bar to grab a coffee.

With one glass of champagne under my belt, I can't afford to further dull my senses, not if I'm going to win bragging rights—and the Master of The Cubeiverse T-shirt I've had my eye on since word of the party popped into my social media feed.

I'm leaning into the bar, shamelessly offering a glimpse of cleavage in hope of luring the busy bartender my way, when I hear it.

The voice.

A rich, deep, sexy-as-hell British voice asking for a Scotch on the rocks.

It's a voice made to melt panties and weaken resolve. That alone is nearly enough to make me rethink my vow to remain married to my pie shop and leave dating to women with more tolerance for assholes and their feathered friends.

I shift to my right, sneaking a peek at the owner of the voice, and I am...lost.

Utterly lost, helpless to resist the magnetic pull of a thirtysomething, dark-haired man with Henry Cavill broad shoulders, the profile of a Roman warrior, a beard I want to feel against my face, and the plushest lips I've ever seen on a man, perfectly full and absolutely kissable. And on this massive, sexy beast in a three-piece suit—clearly custom made to accommodate his staggering broad-shoulder-to-trim-waist ratio—that mouth is perfect.

He's perfect.

And just like that, I decide that he *will* be mine.

At least for a night.

Tonight, I will claim Rubik's Cube victory *and* the pleasure of this gorgeous human's company. Tonight, Gigi James is coming out on top.

Or on top *and* bottom *and* up against the wall *and* as many other positions as we can fit in between now and tomorrow morning.

2

WEST

I didn't come to this party to meet a woman.

I'm here because my friend Graham texted me earlier today. *It'll be fun*, he said. *You can't spend all your time in the States with your nose in your business. Plus, it's a great way to say an ironic 'see you later' to all those dating games.*

With that closing argument, I was sold. Dating shouldn't be a game, but lately I've run into more than my share of women playing the *prove yourself to me* game, *the hard-to-get* game, and the *if he texts first, he's a chump* game.

For fuck's sake—how is that even a thing?

Yet, it is.

Since I'm so very done with figurative games, I said yes to real ones.

But right now, all I want to say is "Hello cleavage. So lovely to make your acquaintance."

To think I nearly missed this chance encounter. If I'd sidled up to this bar a few minutes earlier, I might have missed this beauty in the purple dress—a dress that suggests the *how does one get a woman out of a dress with so many tiny buttons and buckles* game.

Thank you, kismet, for ensuring I was waylaid by an old schoolmate who's still deep in the investment banking scene. I haven't seen Nigel since uni, but he couldn't wait to tell me how much money he was making and to flaunt his Vacheron Constantin watch as we chatted.

He almost clocked me in the nose with it. Twice.

Yes, I get it. You spent nearly $200,000 on a wristwatch. Good on you. And your wife just bought a Bentley.

Or perhaps it was a designer hedgehog. I can't remember, and it hardly matters.

There's a reason I rarely spend time with people who are obsessed with making money.

They're dull.

But gamers? And not just any gamers, but vintage gamers? These are my people, and games belong at a party.

Graham's off with his wife playing Jenga, which I think is a euphemism for foreplay. But with the two of them, everything is a euphemism for foreplay, as it should be when you're disgustingly happily married.

But that's all for the best since here I am face-to-face with the most stunning woman I've seen in ages. I hope she's brainy too.

I noticed her the moment she walked in—the way she owned the room, the confidence in her stride, and in her smile too. A woman who's unafraid to come to a party solo—that's so damn sexy.

Like the rest of her—her curves, her smooth, creamy skin displayed by that fantastic dress with a bustier that's doing everything a bustier should do.

Boost the assets.

All the assets. If they aren't each an overflowing handful, I'll eat my pocket handkerchief.

Her hair tumbles in soft, auburn waves over her shoulders, and her blue eyes shine with shameless appreciation as she meets my gaze, as if she's just tasted the most delicious treat.

It's a damn good look on her.

Especially when the tip of her tongue flicks out to lick the corner of her glossy pink lips, ever so briefly.

Yep, I'm not going anywhere else tonight. She's where I want to spend the rest of the evening. Especially when I notice her earrings, and just like that, I know we have something in common.

With an elbow against the bar, I lock eyes with her, savoring the twinkle in hers. "I hope I'm not being presumptuous, but if you're in need of a Rubik's Cube partner, I can finish in under a minute."

My opening line is a thrown gauntlet, and her lips curve up into a grin I want to kiss. "Well, what do you know? So can I," she says. "Though I'm pretty sure that's the *only* time when finishing in under a minute is something to boast about."

"Exactly. I'm all for endurance and stamina in other areas. Like…swimming, for example," I deadpan.

"Or reading?" she tosses back.

I tap my chin, considering. "Yes. A long read is a

lovely thing. Or perhaps a twenty-four-hour ballroom dancing competition?"

She brings her hand to her chest, fingers splayed across the beautiful cleavage I can't wait to worship with my mouth. "You're speaking my language, mister. Those are some of my very favorite things. But I do believe you left out one important activity that requires stamina."

I knock back some of my Scotch. "Ah, but did I? Perhaps I was simply being polite."

"There's no need for that. Especially since you say you have," she waggles her fingers, her nails decorated in a bright ruby red, and whispers, "magic hands."

Any cuber worth his salt should possess those.

"Oh, I absolutely do."

The bartender hands her a coffee with a, "Here you go. Black and strong."

She flashes him a grin. "Thank you. The only way to drink it."

I beg to differ. The best way to drink coffee is to...*not* drink it. Ever. It's a wretched beverage, but now is not the time to say so.

She lifts the mug and takes a swallow, leaving behind an imprint of her gorgeous lips on the white stoneware. When she sets it on the edge of the bar, my eyes stray to the marks. "Lucky mug."

"I could say the same about your glass of scotch, Mister Magic Hands."

"I'll gladly accept that nickname."

She takes another sip as she looks me over, drinking me in as seductively as she drinks her coffee. I feel like

I'm being sized up for possible devouring and, holy hell, I like it.

With a satisfied sigh, she sets down the mug again. "I think our game of choice requires a certain amount of magic, don't you?"

"Absolutely. Assuming we're here, then, for the same game? What with your earrings, I assumed..." I gesture in the direction of the little Rubik's Cubes hanging from her ears.

She reaches for one, running a finger over the miniature cube in her right lobe, as if she just remembered it's there. "You assume correctly," she says, then lowers her hand.

I eye her up and down, appreciating her attention to detail. Something about the way she's put together —the thick curls of hair, the flouncy dress with all those buttons, the heels, and the charm necklace— suggests she likes looking good for herself, not for a man.

Aside from the cleavage, it's not an outfit designed to attract a man's attention—it's a little too fluffy, too girly, too quirky in a way that reminds me of my sister playing dress up in our mother's closet when we were kids—and that's precisely why it draws my eye.

It says more than *look at me.*

It says she's a woman who knows what she likes, what she wants. Seeing as I'm a man who also knows what he wants—a woman who's as smart and independent as she is sexy—I don't plan on letting this one out of my sight tonight.

"But if you don't want to go cube to cube, we could

always play Scrabble, instead," I suggest. "Keep things friendly."

She leans a little closer and brings her finger to her lips. "Shh. Don't tell anyone, but I'm absolutely down for a game of dirty Scrabble, but only if you show me what you can do with these first," she says, casting a pointed glance down to my hands.

Hell, yes. The game is on, and it's exactly the kind of game I live to play.

I knock back the rest of my Scotch. "I'd love to show you. Any chance you'd like to be my partner in the Rubik's Cube tournament?"

With narrow eyes, she shoots back, "Maybe. But how do I know you won't be the weak link?"

I step closer, hooking a finger gently in one of her curls. "There's nothing weak about me, love."

She shudders. Her breath catches. "All right. Let's go add your name to my team. I signed up for the second heat."

"Perfect." I extend a hand and add, "I'm West, by the way."

When she takes my hand, something shivers up my arm. I don't want to say a spark zaps between us. A spark is just static electricity, and static electricity is unpleasant. But touching this gorgeous woman, even for something as pedestrian as a handshake, is…electric.

"I'm Gigi," she purrs.

I eye her up and down once more. Her purple dress. Her shoes decorated with comic-book drawings of Wonder Woman, Cat Girl and a mélange of female superheroes. The apple pie charm necklace that rests between the tops of her breasts. "You couldn't be anything but a Gigi."

She flashes an absolutely fantastic grin that makes my skin sizzle. "You get me, I think."

Even this woman's smile turns me on.

Whatever game we're playing right now, she's winning and that's fine by me.

* * *

Her fingers fly as she leads off the first round for our team of two, starting by lining up the white center then twisting with rocket speed to make a white cross.

Naturally. That's the only way to start.

She shifts another threesome clockwise, then the next one counterclockwise. I glance at the timer, where the second hand ticks mercilessly.

"Go on—you've got this," I say.

But she needs no encouragement. She's a natural, and I'm enthralled with her play.

Her moves are mesmerizing, her fingers a blur, her eyes intensely focused. In forty-five seconds, the puzzle is gorgeously solid on all six sides. Gigi thrusts it victoriously above her head, then sets it down on the gaming table, smugly triumphant.

"Done. In less than a minute," she says with a flutter of her long lashes.

I high-five her, since that's what you do here in the States. "Nothing sexier than that."

She arches a brow. "Really? Nothing? Are you sure about that, West?"

Oh, she gives good dirty banter, and I lower my voice to a smoky whisper. "Right. You have me there. Nothing sexier…with clothes on, anyway."

"I beg to differ." She shrugs one bare shoulder, in a deliciously coquettish move. "Sometimes it's even more fun with clothes on, shoved aside because you just can't wait those few extra minutes…"

A groan escapes my lips. This woman owns her sexuality, no doubt about it.

I clear my throat. "I concede. That *is* sexier." I hold her gaze for a second, savoring the glimmer in her eyes —the invitation written clearly in them.

But the moment ends when the game master shouts. "Teams four, eight, twelve, sixteen, eighteen, twenty-one, twenty-three, and twenty-six—congratulations, you will advance to round two."

He slams the bell and it's my turn.

Wasting no time, I grab the next cube on the edge of the stage in front of us. The pattern of colored squares may seem frustratingly random, but I see possibilities and permutations, and they unfurl before my eyes. I tackle the cube as I have since I was a kid. Intent on the puzzle, I move the sections around and around, making the orange face, the red one, and so on. In fifty seconds, I'm done.

"Wow," Gigi breathes.

"I told you." I blow on my fingers. "Under a minute."

She hums appreciatively. "And to think I doubted you."

"Did you really?"

She spreads her hands in front of her, a shrug of

admission. "Men like to brag, West, but don't always come through. But looks like you deliver the goods."

Delivering the goods is exactly what I'd like to do with this puzzle-solving, bustier-wearing spitfire of a woman.

"What do you say we lay a wager on the next round?" I ask. "See which one of us solves it faster."

She arches a brow, seeming intrigued. "What exactly do you have in mind, Mr. Sexy English Cuber Magic Hand Man?"

And that seals the deal for me. Any woman who can make a seven-word nickname sound that sexy isn't one you let slip through your fingers.

"I lose, I buy you a drink at the bar down the street."

She cocks her head. "And if I win?"

"I buy you a drink at the bar down the street."

"Well, it sounds like I've already won, then," she says with a slow smile.

Or maybe…we both have.

3

GIGI

There has to be something terribly wrong with this man.

He's probably an axe murderer.

Or he eats sardines for every meal.

Or he trims his toenails with his teeth.

Whatever it is, it must be truly heinous. There's no other explanation for why this buff, bearded, brilliant, and naughty man hasn't already been snapped up by an equally magnificent woman.

Or maybe he's just a serial cheater and a commitment-phobe like all the other men you liked enough to go out with more than once.

Like Nelson, a Manhattan divorce attorney who barked orders at his minions but whispered sweet nothings to me. I stupidly ignored his I-treat-underlings-odiously side. Should have listened to my gut, since he turned out to be odious on every side. Not only did he refuse to ever come to Brooklyn to see me, he also cheated with a client of his, a woman who owns a button shop in the East Village where I sometimes ventured when I needed the perfect button for a vintage ensemble.

Suffice it to say, I do not frequent her shop anymore.

But Odious Nelson and his Buttonista are the past, and I mean to enjoy the hell out of my present.

Meeting West's gaze over our Scrabble board, I smile. Silly brain, it doesn't matter what's wrong with him or if he lives to cheat.

This isn't the start of a beautiful relationship.

This is one night with a magnetic man who's made me smile more in an hour than I have in months.

Genuinely smile, I mean. At Sweetie Pies, I'm all over the customer service smile—I have one of the best in the business, if I do say so myself—but it's been a long time since I felt so...fizzy inside. So excited and eager and filled with anticipation.

It's just so easy to be with this beautiful Brit.

Maybe that's what's wrong with him. Maybe he's only here on vacation...

"There," he says, laying down his tiles. "It isn't as dirty as I'd like, but the letters aren't playing nice with me this round."

"Quiz." I nod in approval as I add to his point column on our sheet of scrap paper. "Twenty-two points. If you can't be dirty, go for the high score."

"Precisely what I was thinking. Though, I think you should get extra points for *nookie*."

"Thanks, but I don't need pity points," I say breezily. "I'll beat you again fair and square."

He chuckles. "I already owe you two drinks. At this rate we'll both be sauced before the end of the night."

I beat his best time at Rubik's Cube—securing our team the title and a pair of matching T-shirts—and tromped him in our first round of Scrabble. But he doesn't seem at all miffed by having his fine ass handed to him. Yet another point in his favor. Sore losers are so irritating, but so many men just can't stand losing, especially to a woman.

"Well," I say as I select my tiles for maximum point damage, "there are worse ways to end an evening."

"Says the woman drinking black coffee all night," he teases.

"Just keeping my wits about me," I murmur. "For now. So, when do you fly home?" I add casually, as if I couldn't care less that he's from a foreign country far, far away.

"No need to fly. I'm in Brooklyn. Just bought a place near the Church Street Station."

I resist the urge to be giddy about the fact that he's a twelve-minute walk across the park from my place—eight if I skip the entire way.

This man makes me feel like skipping.

Which is dangerous, not to mention the opposite of sexy.

Men don't like women who skip, even if their boobs are exceptionally bouncy while they're doing it. Men like women who are serious or sarcastic or glamorous or, at the very least, *not* silly. I learned that the hard way after I zoomed down the slide on Governor's Island— New York's longest—giggling like a madwoman the entire way, and found Theodore waiting at the bottom with a pained, embarrassed expression.

He did not find my whimsy charming.

He found it so un-charming, in fact, that he broke up with me two days later.

So, now, instead of giving in to giddiness, I hum beneath my breath, my focus on the board. "Nice. You're close, then. You won't even need an Uber to get home after I drink you under the table."

He laughs that husky, delicious laugh of his. "Is everything a competition with you?"

"You started it." I peer up at him through my lashes. "And no, I'm not all that competitive, really. Just with games. And work. And girlfriends."

"You're competitive with your friends? How so?" he asks, then adds more cautiously, "Like...which of you makes the most money or something?"

"No, nothing like that," I scoff. "I'm not competitive *with* them. I'm competitive about being their favorite. I want them to like me more than any of their other best girls." I lift two fingers pinched close together. "Just a little bit more."

West hums. "Interesting. And why is that, do you think?"

I bob a shoulder, wishing I hadn't confessed that last bit. I don't want to get up close and personal with this man, I just want to ride him all night like the roller-coaster at Coney Island.

But there's no way to steal the words back, so I figure I might as well answer honestly. "I just love them so much. Adore them, really. They're such clever, kind, creative, funny people. It feels good to be special to someone like that."

"So, which friend do *you* like the best?"

I blink, horrified at the thought. "None of them. I like them all exactly the same. My heart has room for dozens of favorites." I see his point and wrinkle my nose at his smug—but still oh-so-handsome—grin. "Right. Thank you for your insight, Mr. Magic Hands. But I think you should pay less attention to the conversation and more to your final word score." I place my tiles and glance up at him with a triumphant grin.

"Zax," he reads with a heavy sigh.

"It's a—"

"Tool for trimming and puncturing roof slates. Yes, I know. I've played that a time or two myself." He cracks his knuckles. "Nineteen points to you. Which means I need a solid fifteen or more for my next word or I'll never catch up."

"It's all on the line now," I say breathlessly.

It's ridiculous to be turned on because he knows the definition of "zax." Or because he can do math in his head, and quickly too.

But *hello,* tingles running down my spine.

A man who knows his numbers just rings my bell.

"Time to do or die," he agrees. He plucks two tiles from his own tray and lays them down next to my *Z* without breaking eye contact.

Cheeks flushing, I glance down to see he's played "zek" and whisper, "An inmate at a Soviet labor camp."

He makes a soft, almost pained sound beneath his breath, and I look up, nipples tightening in my bustier as his gaze bores into mine. "You are...the sexiest woman I've ever met. I concede."

"You can't concede," I say, fighting a smile. "I haven't beaten you yet."

"Oh yes, you have. I'm utterly destroyed," he murmurs. "And there's only one thing that might ease my suffering."

"And that is?" I arch a brow, electricity dancing over my skin as he takes my hand across the board.

"You. Me. Dark corner booth at the bar. Bourbon apple ciders with extra whipped cream. On me."

My brain conjures an image of West naked, with whipped cream topping the part of him I can't wait to get my hands—and my mouth—on. I smile what I'm sure is a wicked grin. Absolutely positively wicked.

And excited.

And oh-so-ready to be somewhere dark and cozy with this man.

"That sounds perfect." I give his fingers a squeeze. "Just let me settle my tab, and I'll be ready to go."

"No, I'll settle it," he says. "I'm paying tonight. One of the perks of victory."

As a successful business owner, I can absolutely pay for my own coffee and spiked cider—and anything else I need, for that matter—but it's been ages since a man offered to treat me. Every guy I've dated recently prefers to split the check or let me pay, something I always offer to do if I'm the one to suggest the restaurant or bar.

If West wants to pamper me a little, I won't object. "All right. Thank you. I like perks."

"Good, because the perks are just getting started," he says with a wink that would seem cheesy from any other guy.

But this man can pull off a wink, wear the hell out of a suit, and master a Rubik's Cube. Plus, he knows all the high-scoring Scrabble words by heart. Maybe I *am* going to ride a unicorn tonight. A hot, bearded unicorn.

As I watch him walk to the bar, I decide that, with a backside like that, he could probably pull off just about anything. And of course, to me, his nerdy side is nearly as attractive as his drop-dead sexy exterior and swoon-worthy accent.

Nearly.

West pays the check, returns my un-swiped credit card, and pulls my chair out in a display of manners that's also sexy as hell. If he offers his arm and insists I walk on the side of the street farthest from the curb as we transition to the bar, I might faint.

Or spontaneously orgasm.

Preferably the latter.

Wait. Nope. I don't want to trip the light fantastic on a street. I'll faint, have him catch me, and when I come to in the middle of his bed, he'll deliver multiples.

He *is* good at math after all.

He pushes my chair in and nods toward the stage. "I need to say goodbye to my friends before we leave. Want to come?"

I blink and suck in a breath. "You have friends here? God, I'm so sorry. They must think I'm awful, monopolizing you for the entire night."

He smiles as he takes my hand, sending another

sizzle up my arm. "Not at all. They're newlyweds. Repulsively in love. Barely notice if there's anyone else in the room. You know the type."

I laugh. "I do, actually. But I'll wait by the door if that's okay. I need to hit the ladies before we leave."

"All right," he says, releasing my hand with a squeeze. "See you in a bit, then, Gigi."

"In a bit, West," I echo and head to the line for the restroom, even though I don't really need to go.

Meeting his friends might make this feel like more than an easy, breezy thing, and I don't want that. I don't want to feel stressed or nervous or pressured to score another date. I've had enough of that. I simply want to be in the moment and enjoy tonight.

And if it leads to something more than a night...well, that would be nice, I guess. But if it doesn't, I'm okay with that too, as long as I get to play naked Twister with West while I have the chance.

Or naked dominoes. Or naked poker.

As long as we're naked, I'm guessing any game we play will be ten times as fun.

4

WEST

In the main gaming room, I peer over Graham's shoulder as he rolls the die onto the Clue board—Cluedo in the UK—at the high table.

"I vote for Miss Scarlett. It's always Miss Scarlett," I whisper unhelpfully. "With the candlestick."

Graham sears me with a look.

His wife tsks. "West, don't give it away. Graham is just learning how to play Clue."

I jerk my head back. "You don't know how to play Clue?"

"I know how. I'm just not obsessed with board games like *some people*," my American friend says, pretending to search for someone in the crowd.

"No idea who you might mean."

"Also, I prefer strip Clue," he mutters as he moves his game piece to the library.

"Sweetheart, you wouldn't be any better at that," CJ says sympathetically then adopts a cheery grin. "Which means we should go home and play right now."

Graham shifts to her side of the standing table to loop an arm around her waist. "And it'll be my wife in the kitchen with *my* candlestick."

She swats his shoulder as I roll my eyes. "Like I told my new friend—*revoltingly in love*, you two." That gets CJ's attention. "Is the new friend of the female variety?"

"Yes. A lovely, brilliant one. We're off to grab a nightcap."

Graham points to the door. "Why the hell are you talking to us, then? Get out of here."

"Just letting you know I'm taking off."

CJ shoos me with both hands. "And now you may go. Be on your way."

"So much for manners," I say.

CJ scoffs. "No need for niceties when there's love in the air."

"Love?" I voice the four-letter word like it tops the lot of them. Because it does, along with *tuna* and *iron*. If I never eat sushi or flatten my own shirt collar again, I'll consider myself a lucky man. "No, none of that nonsense. Just a good time with a great woman. See you two later."

The last time I felt the inklings of something *more than like*, I learned Olivia was only interested in a five-letter word. *Money*. Another reason why I have no patience for dating games.

When I leave The Library, I find Gigi outside leaning against the brick wall, holding her phone out in front of her, arm outstretched.

Is she taking a selfie?

Odd.

Despite the showy clothes, she doesn't seem like an Instagrammer. A selfie seems against her code.

If pressed, I would have said selfies were beneath her.

But maybe I'm doing that thing again, that thing where I think better of people than they deserve. I'd hoped to leave that habit behind me in London.

Gigi turns her gaze to me, laughs, then rolls her eyes as she waggles the phone. "I was trying to make the font smaller. I have this friend who sends me drafts of her sexy short stories to read for feedback. But they're in twenty-point font. I have to scroll every other sentence."

"That's quite a large font."

She gives an approving nod. "Yes, it is. I'm generally good with...large things. But I like to tease Rosie about being a Gigantic Font Whore. She teases back, saying I'll be grateful for anything gigantic in my life when I'm her age." She adds in a confiding stage whisper, "Though at fifty I'm pretty sure she's getting more action than all of my other friends put together. Her blog is scandalous."

"Really? How so?" I ask, fascinated by this woman and her...*zest*.

"She writes all about her big city Sexcapades. In depth. No subject is taboo. I'll shoot you a link and you can read for yourself."

"Or maybe you could read me an excerpt or two? I'm guessing you're great at reading aloud, what with your mastery of Z-words and all." I lower my voice and set a hand on the small of her back. It's the perfect fit. And even better? The way she shivers and shifts closer when I touch her.

Thank you again, kismet. There's nothing hotter than a responsive woman, and Gigi is like a cat who arches into my touch, who savors and purrs for it.

Meow.

"All right. Here's a snippet. 'It was a hot sticky night in the city and all the zeks were out wielding their zaks, hoping to get off work early and get lucky,'" she whispers in a narrator voice.

I hum low in my throat. "Raunchy things, those zeks."

"Very much so," she says. "Into handcuffs and scarves too, I hear. When they don't have a zak in hand."

"Scarves you say..." I tap my temple, filing the breadcrumb she's dropped. "Noted. Now I have a most important question," I say as we walk to Camp Whiskey.

"I'm all ears."

"These T-shirts." I point to them, draped over her arm. "I feel it's important we wear them out in public as soon as possible, so that everyone we meet can admire and envy our accomplishment. But I'm torn. If you were to put one on, it would ruin the stunning view I've been enjoying all night."

She presses her hand to her chest, faux shocked. "Were you checking out my décolletage?"

"Guilty."

She grins, a naughty glint in her eye as she rolls her index finger at my pecs. "Then you should definitely atone by taking off your fancy clothes and wearing a T-shirt instead."

"What the woman wants..."

As we amble down the block, I go with it, shrugging

out of my jacket. I hook it over my arm and begin to unbutton my shirt.

Her blue eyes go wide, traveling lasciviously down my chest as I loosen the buttons. I get to the last one and tug the shirt out of my trousers. Then I shed it too.

She blinks, drops her jaw, makes a show of lifting it again with two fingers under her chin. "Wow."

I chuckle, pleased she likes the view, and hand her my jacket and shirt. When I've pulled on the T-shirt, I take back my clothes and then square my shoulders, preening for her benefit. "There you go, madam."

She sighs. "No. See, now you've gone and ruined everything, West."

"You prefer the dress shirt?"

"I prefer *no* shirt," she says with an adorable pout.

"Well, I think I can make that happen. Later," I say as we reach the door to Camp Whiskey. "For now, shall we find a booth and talk some more?"

"Yes. *Talk*," she purrs, having fun with the word, as if she knows that it's just another word for foreplay.

With her? It absolutely is.

* * *

First, I pop into the lav to wash up. It would be rude to touch her after I've had my hands on all those cubes and Scrabble tiles, and since I fully intend to have my hands on her, I do the gentlemanly thing.

I return to the booth, sliding in next to her beneath wooden cutouts of bears rowing boats and lolling in tree branches. Camp Whiskey has a rustic lodge invaded by kitsch vibe I enjoy and an unparalleled selection of whiskey and scotch. Even the speakeasy in the Village where I occasionally spend a lazy Sunday afternoon playing cards with Graham can't compare.

"This is my favorite part of Brooklyn," Gigi declares, smoothing her dress. "All the space. I can't get away with a crinoline in Manhattan."

I cast a glance at the flouncy skirt currently occupying its own zip code between us.

She reaches for the fabric, folding it over her leg on one side. "Or...maybe not?"

I slide my hand down her arm, enjoying the way she leans into my touch. "What do you take me for? A man who doesn't know what he wants?"

"What do you mean?" Her question is a little breathy, a little distracted.

From my fingers trailing down her bare skin.

Good.

"I asked you out for a drink. Of course, I want to sit right next to you. Not at a respectable, giant-skirt distance."

She dips her head, looking the tiniest bit shy, then raises her eyes, nibbling on the corner of her lip. "I like a man who knows his mind."

"You've found one."

The waitress arrives and takes our drink order, and as soon as she leaves, I return my focus to Gigi. My fingers travel up her shoulder, over her neck, under her hair.

"Mmm," she murmurs.

Gently, I play with her hair. "What else do you love about Brooklyn?"

She takes a beat, arching into my touch—she really might be part feline. "Oh, so many things. The architecture and the artsy vibe and how close we are to the shore for swimming in the summer. Coney Island, even though it's tacky. And all the different kinds of people and food and music venues and shopping. We have the most eclectic and exciting shops in the world, I think. Though, I haven't been many other places."

"Where else can you find a pickle shop next to a purveyor of handmade pork pie hats."

Her eyes light up. "Yes! Exactly."

I let my gaze roam down to her eclectic, exciting dress. "And you look like you fit right in here."

"Thanks. But that makes sense—I've been here my whole life."

My brows lift. "Really? That's rare, isn't it? I haven't met many Brooklyn natives."

"A rare breed, spotted in the wild," she says as the waitress returns with our bourbon and ciders. No whipped cream—alas, they were out—but I'm still looking forward to tasting cinnamon and clove on Gigi's lips later.

But hopefully not too much later.

Anticipation is all part of the fun, but the more time I spend with this woman, the more I want to see more of her. All of her.

I lift my glass to toast, and she raises hers.

"What shall we toast to?" I ask, hoping she'll pick something wicked. Or at least wanton.

"Gentlemen's choice," she counters, ever the worthy opponent.

Fine by me. I know exactly what I want. "Let's drink to the best kind of games."

"And those are?"

I lean close, brush a soft curl of her hair off her shoulder, then press a kiss to the column of her throat. "Bedroom games, of course."

She trembles, her next breath releasing in a soft whoosh.

"I think I like those kinds of games," she says as I pull back, and we clink glasses.

"Think? Or know?"

She takes a sip of her cider, moaning soft appreciation for the spicy, fragrant concoction. "I think it depends on the player, don't you?" she asks in a whisper that sends darts of heat down my spine.

Her voice. Her boldness. Mixed with that faint touch of submission. I don't go looking for submission. But I'm a firm believer in listening to a woman, then giving her what she wants. And if she wants me to lead, then I'll do just that.

But a man should always ask. "I have one more thing I'd like to toast to."

"*Multiple* toasts," she says musing on the first word. "That sounds promising."

"I always deliver on my promises," I knock back some bourbon, savoring the cider and the burn.

"Let's find out." She tilts her chin just so, offering those gorgeous lips and I take the gift of her mouth.

I slide my lips across hers, a gentle sweep at first,

tasting the cinnamon and apple of the drink and a hint of vanilla I'm guessing is her lipstick. I inhale the scent of her hair, letting the flowers and sweet spice go to my head. My mind becomes a haze of her lips and her soft murmurs.

I cup her cheek in my hand, stroking my thumb gently across her soft skin as I press my lips a little harder, kiss a little deeper, exploring her delicious mouth. A moan seems to fall unbidden from her and she arches even closer. With her hip against mine, her hand drifts up my chest, making my skin heat.

I kiss her more deeply, tongues stroking, mouths discovering, breath mingling. Her moans and sighs are shameless and real, and I love them. Love hearing how much I affect her. Love too that her hand travels briefly across my beard, then grips the fabric of my shirt as she pulls me closer, making her wishes known.

Making it clear that this doesn't need to be a careful kiss.

I rope a hand into her hair, threading through the strands, then giving a gentle tug, just to see how she responds. A small catch of her breath, followed by a husky moan of approval, is the answer.

The perfect answer.

I break the kiss, and she looks up at me, lust drunk. "Do that again? Please?" she says.

"I'd like to do all sorts of things to you."

"Like…my favorite things?" she asks, both flirty and dirty.

"If your favorite things include coming. A lot."

Her eyes twinkle. "However did you know?"

"Lucky guess. I hope that's not too forward," I say playfully, though I suspect I know the answer.

She tap-dances her fingers up my chest. "Oh, I like forward. I like it a lot."

"Good to know." My fingers drift down, down, into the darkness under the table to the hem of her skirt. "Let's see how I do in the first heat of the coming competition," I say, then coast a hand under her skirt, up her leg, on the fast track for my favorite place.

She moans before I even touch her.

"But you're going to have to be quiet," I murmur into her ear. "If you keep making all these delicious, attention-grabbing noises I'll have to stop."

She shakes her head. "No. Don't stop," she whispers, as my hand reaches the apex of her thighs.

I bite my lip as I feel the cotton panel of her knickers, how damp it is, how aroused she is. My fingers travel to the waistband, slipping under it, over her curls, then between her legs, where they glide across that glorious slickness.

She shudders, a beautiful, silent shudder that sends a tremor of lust down my spine.

My cock hardens as I trace all that silky wetness. Gigi trembles as I touch her, her hand gripping my arm, like she needs desperately to hold on to something. To me.

She parts her legs, widening them, giving me more access.

I stroke faster, focusing my attention on that swollen bundle of nerves that's pulsing, begging for touch.

Touch I'm all too happy to provide.

Her other hand grips the edge of the table, as she clamps her lips shut. Sparks sizzle across my skin as I watch her face. As I memorize the way her forehead furrows as her breath comes fast, then faster still.

As her face becomes a map of exquisite torture.

But the whole while, she remains quiet. Like a good dirty girl. "That's right. Don't let anyone hear you," I whisper. "If anyone hears, I'll have to stop."

A soft whimper falls from her lips but then she purses them.

Dipping my face to her neck, I whisper against her skin, "So good. Just like that."

I stroke faster, sliding a finger inside her sweet center and crooking it, hitting that spot inside her that makes her thighs clench, and her breath stutter.

"Ohhh, West," she gasps. My name on her lips is filthy and needy. It sends the desire in me spiking higher, then higher still as she begs "Don't stop."

Such a beautiful beggar.

As if I could stop.

I have only one choice now. To seal my mouth to hers and cover her lips with a kiss as she trembles, her body shaking, as my gorgeous stranger comes for the first time tonight.

If I have my way, it won't be the last.

And I intend to have my way with her.

Once she's stopped trembling, I wipe my hand on a cloth napkin, press another kiss to her lips, and reach for my glass.

Down the hatch.

"Now, shall we get started on number two straightaway?"

"I don't want another drink," she says.

"I wasn't talking about the drink."

Her swollen lips curve up at the edge. With glassy eyes and flushed cheeks, she nods. "Yes, please," and I lift my hand for the check.

5

GIGI

Sex plans are full of awkward moments.

This is the "my place or yours" dilemma. Or, as I like to call it, "if he turns out to be crazy am I more likely to be murdered at my place or his?"

I don't seriously believe I'm going to be murdered tonight, but it's a consideration for women—hence the baseball bat under my bed. I believe in listening to my gut. And my gut says that the only thing West is likely to kill is my bad luck streak with men.

He's just so delightful in every way.

"I'm a fifteen-minute walk away," I offer as we tumble out of Camp Whiskey. "Give or take ten minutes to rest if my heels start hurting."

"I'll call an Uber."

A few minutes later, we slide into the back of the car.

On the drive, he's all hands and dirty talk. His fingers glide up my neck, threading through my hair. "I'd really like to put you on your knees," he murmurs in my ear.

That sends a ribbon of heat down my body. "So I can suck your cock?" I ask under my breath. I'm helpful like that.

"I like the way you think, but I'm not that selfish. I want you to ride me first, then I'd like to put you on your hands and knees so I can fuck you hard and deep, make you come over and over. And I'd really like to smack your ass as I take you over the edge."

Unicorn. Called it. He is officially a sex unicorn.

And I'm going to ride him and play with that golden horn all night long.

"Are we adding mind-reader to the list of skills you've mastered?" I ask.

He grins, all wicked and sly. "No, but I can read your body language. You're a woman who likes to have fun, who likes to feel good, and who deserves to be the center of attention. And your orgasm will be the star of the show tonight."

"Will it make multiple appearances?"

"It'll take encores."

"Standing ovations too." I don't know that I can bear this arousal as the car cruises the final block to my apartment. I might melt into a lust puddle before I get upstairs.

But somehow, I'll manage. I haven't roped a unicorn only to lose him now.

When we reach my building, West thanks the driver, and we get out. I unlock the front door quickly. My hands shake slightly, but not from fear. From excitement.

Is it just the prospect of hot, sweaty, up-against-the-wall, bent-over-the-bed, upside-down sex?

Well, yes.

But there's more to it. When I told West, "You get me," before the cubing competition, I meant it playfully. Only now it seems he *does* get me. We vibe. We're in synch. He's like the ideal dance partner in my ballroom class. In a few short hours, we've clicked in a way I haven't clicked with anyone in too long. I can't help thinking this might be more than the no-strings hookup I imagined when I first spotted him at the bar.

I mean, how often do you meet a man who makes your mind tingle every bit as much as your body?

Shut up, brain, my body shouts. *We're in charge right now. Filthy sex first; romantic daydreams later.*

Yes, body. *You're coming in loud and clear.*

I briefly consider taking the steps two at a time, but my heels forbid it.

Also, I don't want to appear overeager.

But who am I kidding? West knows how eager I am to get naked and shameless with him.

Then we're inside, and the door snicks shut. It's the sound of the first half of the evening ending and the second half beginning.

That's what tonight feels like. A beginning.

West holds my face, two big hands clasping my cheeks, his dark brown eyes holding mine.

"I've changed my mind," he declares.

What? No!

"Why?" I ask, my voice pitching up.

"You're so unbelievably sexy we have to start with *me* on my knees."

"Oh." I blink. And smile. And whisper, "Proceed."

West moves at lightning speed. He drops to his knees, pushes my skirt and the crinoline underneath up to my waist, then tugs my panties down my legs. I've barely stepped out of them when his mouth is on me.

And dear God.

I melt in seconds.

My hands fly to his hair as I gasp, "Oh, God."

His tongue slides along my slickness, lapping me up, tasting me. Add in that scratch of his beard, and I am a happy camper. Oh yes, I am. He licks soft and tender at first, just the way I like it. My moans seem to lead him on, and he picks up the pace. Masterful with his lips, soon he's sucking and nibbling on my clit, driving me wild. As I curl my hands tighter around his head, I thread my fingers through his thick hair, yanking him closer. I lean back against the wall, my spine digging into the plaster.

It hurts, but it's a good kind of hurt, the kind that reminds me how wonderful it is to have my pussy kissed senseless by a stunning British man on his knees.

A man who is utterly devouring me.

I babble incoherently, a string of *oh Gods* and *yeses* that make him moan against me.

He kisses with so much hunger, so much desperation that *his* want flips the switch inside me. Bliss coils tight in my belly then unleashes with a force that makes my bones tremble. I shudder, coming on his lips with a loud *yes, oh God, yes.*

My head is a haze. My chest is heaving. My skin is red-hot as he rises and wipes a hand across his mouth. "You were right. Why bother taking clothes off?"

I gesture to him, making a circle with my finger so I can give an executive order. "Nope. Off. Now. Take off everything now." I reach for his belt but wobble in my shoes. He steadies me, both hands on my hips as I kick off the heels.

"I think I'm a little sex-woozy." More like West-woozy, but at the moment, they're the same.

He drags his lips along my neck, whispering a hot, "Oh no. I hear the only cure is more sex."

"Then, cure me, West."

I lead him to my bedroom, then flick on the light because with a man like West, I don't want to do it in the dark. I want to get frisky with the lights on. I want to see his magnificent body, watch his rippling muscles, gaze at his gorgeous face as he breaks apart.

As he makes me break apart again.

Once in my room, I strip off his shirt. Having fun with his belt, I hum a naughty little tune as I unbuckle it, then slide down his pants. He toes off shoes and socks then works his fingers down the front of my dress. He's quick and adept with all the little buckles and snaps, but he's missing one critical bit of data.

"I'm going to give you a tip, Mister Sexy English Cuber."

He raises his face, tilts his head. "What would that be?"

I spin around. "There's a zipper."

He laughs, and even that's sexy. Husky. Just right.

"Zippers are my new favorite thing," he says, sliding it down notch by delicious notch. The sound of it opening sends a thrill through my body. He guides down the fabric, the straps over my arms, the bodice falling down my waist, then to the floor.

"So beautiful," he says, as he draws a line with his finger along my spine to the top of my ass. "This back is so fucking gorgeous. I want to mark it. With my hands. With my come."

I shudder at the prospect of all those glorious coming opportunities. And I make a mental note that if all goes well, I might even ask him for a repeat because I like the sound of that last dirty one—*a lot.*

Yes, I want more West already. I want another night like this, from the way it started at the bar to the way it's playing out now.

He whirls me around once more and unhooks my bra.

Then it's my turn, and I feel like I'm unwrapping a present. As I reach his boxer briefs, I grin wickedly. They're orange. For some reason, this delights me. Most men wear black or gray. West isn't afraid to don a pair of bright orange boxer briefs, and the color does wonders for his cock.

But then his cock seems to be the eighth wonder of the modern world.

I push his briefs down, gasping as I take in the view of his arousal. He's hard, thick, pulsing. I wrap my fingers around his shaft, and he twitches in my hand.

I grow even wetter. A pulse beats between my legs, and I ache for him.

"Gigi," he rasps out.

"I would like to ride this cock," I say with wicked glee.

"Then cover me up, woman, and get on top."

I hustle over to my nightstand to grab a condom, but the expiration date is not my friend.

"Oh shoot," I say.

"Are they expired?"

"Yes. It's been ages."

He reaches for his wallet in his pants, flicks it open, grabs the protection. Moving to the bed, he settles onto it and slides it down his cock. I climb over him, straddling him.

"Now ride me, gorgeous. Ride me like you've wanted to all night," he says, clutching my hips, lifting me above so I'm poised to drop down on his fantastic erection.

"How do you know I've been wanting to do it all night?"

Brushing a finger along my hip, he levels me with a hot stare. "The way you look at me."

Trembling with pleasure, with anticipation, I ask, "How do I look at you?" I'm shameless with him, but his praise is life. I want to eat it up, drink it down, swallow it whole. His words are sexier than his body, and his body is a work of art.

"The same way I look at you. With white-hot desire," he says, then he grips the base of his dick, rubs it against my wet folds, and pushes up into me.

Oh, hello, Pleasure. It's been a while, but it's so very good to see you again.

It's been so long that it's almost a new sensation, but

I know exactly what to do with it. I set my hands on his pecs, rocking my hips, swaying, swiveling. Finding a pace instantly.

West doesn't look away. He gazes at my face, stroking his thumb over my cheek, giving me compliments, endless compliments.

And I inhale them like oxygen.

"So sexy," he says. A hand slides down my chest, gripping my right breast. Squeezing it.

I bow my back as lust ripples through me.

"Your tits are fucking perfect, Gigi. Such a fantastic handful," he groans, his other hand joining the party.

Squeezing and kneading my breasts as I rise and fall, as I writhe and rock. As we moan and groan together. He's so deep in me, so far, and he fucks up into me, filling me.

His hand coasts lower, over my belly button, his thumb reaching my clit.

The second he touches me, I scream in pleasure.

I'm so sensitive, so aroused already, and as he strokes and rubs, fucks and grinds, I am lost. Lost in the pleasure, just like I was lost in his voice mere hours ago. With his fingers and his cock working in tandem, he coaxes another orgasm out of me as I tremble, shaking, falling apart on my handsome stranger.

Who barely feels like a stranger at all.

He feels like a brand-new lover.

The kind who'll send me dirty missives.

Who'll tell me how much he longed for my body while he was at work, in his corner office, overseeing money or gold or whatever he does in those suits.

Mostly, he feels like the kind of lover who wants more than one time.

That's what I want too.

And I want *more* this very second.

West makes me ravenous, and I'm a greedy woman tonight.

He slides his hands into my hair, pulls my face close to his, and whispers, dark and dirty, "Get on your hands and knees now. I need to fuck you hard and ruthlessly."

"I love ruthless fucking. So much." I slide off him, flipping over and into the position he wants.

He kneels behind me, those big hands curling over my ass, spreading me open. He runs the head of his cock through my wetness and slides back inside, filling me.

It's such a decadent position, such a submissive position. It makes me feel like an animal, and I love it. I love the rawness of it. And I love the way he can own my body like this.

West needs no ownership manual. He knows what to do.

As I lower my chest towards the bed, propped on my elbows, he slides his hand down my spine, towards my neck. He grips my hair and tugs hard as he buries his cock inside me.

He is relentless. Ruthless. Dominating and dirty, as he fucks and fucks and fucks. Grabbing my strands, making me yelp.

He slides his hand the other direction, on a fast-track for my ass, and I turn my face, needing to watch.

"That's right. Watch me, love. Watch as I smack this

beautiful ass," he says, lifting his hand, bringing it down hard on my rear.

I yelp, the pain radiating, morphing into pleasure, incomparable pleasure.

He lifts his other hand, smacks my other cheek, hard and punishing.

"Yes," I whimper into the bed.

"Your skin is so beautiful. It wears my marks so well," he rasps.

"Do it again," I say, urging him on. But he needs no urging.

Another smack. Another sharp zing of pleasure.

The Sex Ninja brings his other hand back to my clit, pinches it, then drives deep inside me.

I am a whimpering mess of pleasure and just the right amount of pain, as my body gives in and I come once again on an epic cry of *oh my God, oh my God, oh my God.*

But this time I'm not alone. This time he joins me with a guttural groan. "So fucking hot," he roars as he unleashes his pleasure, and we fall apart together.

As we pant and moan, he sweeps a kiss across my neck. "And that was the best game of the night."

"Yes." I sigh. "Best. Game. Ever."

Then, he gets up to dispose of the condom in my bathroom and returns seconds later, settling next to me, his warm body snug against mine. Mmm. This feels so good.

This post-sex high.

It makes me picture possibilities.

More nights like this, more moments rich with rata-tat-tat banter, one-up-manship wit, dirty Scrabble. Maybe even Strip Dungeons and Dragons.

Is that a thing?

If not, it should be. I bet West would play it.

I bet he'd love to play it with me.

West is no Theodore. He's no slide-shaming dipshit.

Fine, I've only spent one night with him, but it's been an electric, flirty, and most of all, an *honest* night.

I'm not looking for a boyfriend. I'm not interested in entanglements. I'm not even sure I have room in my life for anything more than Sweetie Pies. But I am very interested in seeing West again.

For more of the same.

Maybe it's the nookie buzz talking, but I don't care.

Sex-drunk and giddy on endorphins, I roam my fingers down his chest. "And we should play it again. Soon," I suggest, nerves fluttering in me.

"We should, and we will."

Why yes, universe, thank you. This was a perfect night.

6

WEST

Best night ever.

This woman is brilliant. Fantastic. Funny.

And sexy as hell.

I don't want the night to end, though I'm usually a big fan of hitting the road after the fun is over so that I can get home, shower, and prepare for an early start in the morning.

But everything is already in place for the grand opening next week. There's not much left to do except stock shelves and arrange the knick-knacks on the walls, and Abby's promised to take care of that on Monday. My sister isn't much use in the kitchen, but when it comes to spiffing up a room, she's an artist. The beautifying of the space is better left in her hands.

So really, I'm free to take a breather for a few days.

A few days I'd really love to stay locked up in my house, in my bed, with this gorgeous creature. Once we're half-dressed and relatively decent, I trap Gigi between my arms against the counter in her tiny kitchen. "Come home with me," I say. "I have so many plans for your beautiful body. And," I say, kissing her jaw, "I might have backgammon."

Her place is adorable—as cute and packed with personality as she is—but I'd love to fuck her on the ladder in my library. And in my giant bathtub upstairs. And in my bed with the thick curtains, we can pull around it to make it night for as long as we like.

"I do love backgammon. And your plans, but I can't," she says with a sigh. "I have so much to do tomorrow."

"Work?" I wrinkle my nose. "Call in sick."

She laughs. "I can't call in sick. I'm the owner, but no, it's not work. Tomorrow's my day off, but I have tons of work things to catch up on here at home. Orders, and paperwork, and all the behind-the-scenes stuff that's not exciting but has to be done."

"Perfect. Bring your behind-the-scenes stuff to my place. I can fuck you gently to sleep and you can work in the morning."

"What if I wanted to be fucked roughly to sleep?" she says in that naughty voice of hers. The one I'm quickly becoming addicted to.

"Even better." I step in, pressing my body against hers, letting her feel how very *up* I am for fucking her any way she wants.

"God, you're tempting." She tilts her head back, moaning softly as she sets her water glass on the counter beside the sink. "But I really can't. I have to visit my grandmother tomorrow too. I've been so busy I haven't seen her in almost two weeks."

"I haven't seen my grandmother in months. I doubt

she's even noticed. Time goes by fast when you're old. Or so she tells me."

Her eyes narrow. "I love Gram. And spending time with her."

"I love my nan too. She's an incredible human, who would completely understand if I needed to have a three day stay at home sex holiday with a beautiful woman instead of coming to play croquet with her on the back lawn. She'd encourage it, in fact."

"Nice. I'd like to dispense sex encouragement when I'm a grandmother. Also, I see we're up to three days now?" Gigi asks with a laugh. She cocks her head, nibbling her lip in that slightly shy way that makes me want to kiss her. But so far, a lot of her mannerisms have that effect on me. "I would love to spend three days in your bed, but…"

"But what?" I ask, easing back a bit, giving her space. There's a serious note in her voice I haven't heard before. Did I read her wrong when she asked for another time? She hesitates and I encourage gently, "Whatever's on your mind, you can tell me. I enjoy honesty outside the bedroom too."

She fiddles with the silky tie on her fluffy feathered robe, the one that makes her look like a 1950's movie star between takes on set. "You're…incredible."

"I was thinking the same about you," I say. "But… I'm definitely hearing a but in there somewhere."

Her lips curve, but her smile fades as she continues, "I want to see you again. I truly do. But I can't steal away for a sex fest, as appealing as that sounds. I can't throw all my responsibilities out the window. I just took over as head of my family's business and I'm in the middle of major renovations. And I checked my email while you were in the bathroom and found out I've been invited to join this super prestigious competition I applied for a few months ago."

"Congratulations," I say, automatically, though I can't help but be concerned that she's back to business so soon after coming her brains out.

I would have assumed she'd need at least a few hours rest to be up to tackling email.

"Thank you." Her hand flutters to brush her hair from her forehead. "I didn't think there was any way I'd get in. It's the first time I've applied, and they usually pick more established people. But I guess they're making a point to give up-and-comers a chance this year so..." She pulls in a bracing breath. "I really need to make the most of this opportunity. I might not get another shot at something like this. Ever. And the first part of the competition starts on Monday. So..."

"You need your beauty sleep."

"Yes," she says. "And probably not to disappear into a gorgeous man's bedroom for three days. Even though I would love to. So, can we take a rain check for the sex fest and make plans for, I dunno, something simpler? But also involving sex, and food, and getting to know you and that naughty mouth of yours."

A woman who knows her limits. A woman who expresses her truth.

I could get used to this. It's unusual, but completely welcome.

"Absolutely." I take her hand and lift it to my lips,

pressing a kiss to her fingers. "I'm busy too. I completely understand."

"But we should definitely do this again," she says, trailing off, like she's leaving me an invitation–to ask her out again.

Or for the first time I should say.

I RSVP.

"Damn straight we should. You can text me when you have an evening free. Or we could grab lunch someday if you like. I'd love to pick your brain about the area. Get the local, inside scoop on the best restaurants, pickle shops, places to buy pork pie hats."

"You'd be hot in pork pie." She smiles, then snags her phone and we exchange numbers. "And I'd love that. How's Wednesday?"

I try to rein in a grin. I'd almost pegged her as the leave 'em hanging type. But here she is making plans before the night is even over. No games, no bullshit. Just boundaries and communication. She is who she is. And I like that. "Wednesday sounds perfect."

"Though a lunch date might not give us enough time for sex," she says with a frown.

"Then on our lunch date, we'll make plans for a steamy night in, instead of this three-day sex fest you declined."

"It pained me to decline," she says, all flirty again. "Seriously. Real, genuine pain."

"Oh, it pained me too. But I plan on teasing you over lunch, getting you all hot and bothered, so you'll be begging for a quickie after the sandwich. How does that sound?"

She sidles up against me. "You're making me hungry." She shifts into a practical mode. "How's eleven on Wednesday? I usually take a lunch break then. Between the morning and the afternoon rush." She motions out the window behind her. "I own Sweetie Pies, the pie shop on the corner."

I startle for a moment, but school my expression.

"How perfect is that?" I ask, a slow grin spreading across my face, suddenly glad I didn't mention the location of *my* new business when we arrived at her apartment.

At the time I hadn't wanted to distract from the pressing business of delivering her second orgasm as soon as possible—or introduce information that might complicate matters later. If the sex had been awful, I figured I could keep an eye on the walk and arrange not to be out and about on the street at the same time as my new neighbor.

But the sex was amazing, and we seem to be on the exact same, low-stress-casual-dating page.

She laughs. "Well, I think it's pretty perfect. It's my baby." She tilts her head, her brow knitting. "But why is that perfect? Have you been in for a slice? Maybe on a Sunday or occasional Monday morning when I wasn't working because, I would have remembered you," she says, wagging a finger.

I smile wider. "No. I haven't been in yet. But I've passed by several times and always admired the cartoon on your sandwich board outside. The curvy woman in the pink dress makes sense now." I roam my gaze over her, the inspiration for the illustration I've had a bit of a thing for.

She rolls her eyes. "Thanks. My cousin drew it. Thought it would be good for branding. So far, she's been right. Online orders are way up since we switched the logo on Valentine's Day this year."

"Brilliant," I say, her words reminding me I should probably have some cute menus designed as well. A minimalist by nature, a heavy cream card stock with daily offerings typed out with my vintage typewriter appeals to my sensibilities, but the customers in this area might expect something more whimsical.

"It's been a great few months." Her gaze flicks down my bare chest to my suit pants and back up again, her naughty grin returning. "And a great night."

"So great," I agree, curling my fingers around her hip and pulling her close.

"You know, just because I can't go home with you," she begins, looping her arms around my neck, "doesn't mean you can't stay the night here if you want. We could sleep in, have lazy morning sex, and when we wake up, we can order pie and coffee delivered from this super cute shop on the corner."

I admit I'm relieved. At first, I thought she was a *see-you-later-er*. Or a *wham bam-thank-you-sir-er*. But what she's describing suits my speed these days.

"Sounds perfect." I cup her ass as I bend, brushing my lips over hers, electricity bristling across my skin as we touch.

And then her scent is flooding my head again— flowers and spice, now with a top note of sex. She smells like a woman who's been thoroughly ravaged, salty and sticky and oh so sweet.

I forget about everything but making her come for me again, this time with her hands braced on the kitchen sink while I play with her tits and take her from behind, whispering filthy things about how good her tight, wet little pussy feels on my cock when I'm fucking her. Promising I'm going to fuck her until she can't stand upright on her own.

And I always keep my promises.

We're up until nearly four a.m., and by the time I wake in the morning, Gigi's gone.

But there's a note on her pink flamingo sheets.

Delivery was going to take 45 minutes, so I ran down the street to get coffee and pie myself. Be back in a jiff. Feel free to leave your clothes off. My coconut cream is delicious licked off all the places I want to lick you. Xo -Gigi

Grinning, I swing my legs out of bed and hurry to throw on my clothes, determined to dash across the street to my shop to grab some tea and be back in this bed naked before Gigi returns.

I adore that woman and can't wait to taste her pie, but I won't drink coffee for anyone—no matter how tight and sweet her pussy or delightful her company.

On a hook in the front hall, I find a key hanging from a Rosie the Riveter keychain. I make sure it works for the front door then take the stairs to the ground floor two at a time.

I'm already across the street—thank you light Sunday morning traffic—and unlocking the shop when the texts start coming in—

shocked emoji face

angry emoji face

head exploding emoji face

GIF of cat hissing at the camera

GIF of woman screaming "betrayed" as she rolls down a hill covered in snow

GIF of a stick-figure man approaching a stick-figure woman with knife, man says "here hold this," stabs knife in girl's stomach, turns and walks away

"What the…" Scowling, I scroll up to the number. The one I entered last night.

My stomach drops.

I look up to see Gigi standing across the street, looking adorable in a pair of red overalls and a white T-shirt with her hair tied up in a red and white polka dot scarf. She has a paper bag, which I assume holds pie, looped over her arm and a cardboard tray with two coffees in one hand. With the other, she's texting a mile a minute.

Texting and glaring at me with murder in her eyes.

7

GIGI

West looks baffled.

Beautiful and baffled, but I'm not buying the innocent act for a second.

No wonder he wanted to steal me away for a sex marathon. To overdose me on orgasms so I wouldn't realize he's the villain who bought the shop across the street.

"What's wrong?" he calls, lifting his phone, his expression confused. "Why are you virtually rolling down a hill covered in snow?"

Ha! As if he doesn't know.

He could have picked any moment between arriving at my place last night and when I promised him pie early this morning to reveal that *he's* the owner of the evil tea shop across the street.

Instead, he kept that information to himself.

Probably so he could spy on me, eat my delicious pie, and steal the recipe. Because if his tongue is half as fluent in pie ingredients as it is in orgasms, reverse engineering by taste would be a snap for him.

I can see it now, his plan to sus out the competition. And I was so clueless and trusting and drunk on orgasms and unicorn peen that I missed the opportunity to take similar advantage of him.

I mean, for research, I could choke down his horrible hard English scones or meat pies or whatever gross thing he's going to sell over there. But I won't have a chance now, will I? Because he lied to me and deceived me, just like every other guy I've seriously dated.

But instead of just wounding my heart, he could have hurt my business. I'm pretty sure I made it crystal clear to him that my business is my *top* priority. So much so that I put work responsibilities ahead of epic sex-fests and magical tongues with pie identification superpowers.

"Please, Gigi." He motions toward the shop behind him. "Is it because of this? If so, I can explain."

"Oh, I'm sure you can." I shoot death rays at him with my eyes, fueled by ravaging hurt and disappointment. "After all, *how perfect is that?*" I pour on a thick English accent, imitating him when he learned I ran Sweetie Pies. "You could have said something then. But nope. You were like *let me show her my perfect cock and my perfect body and my perfect accent and give her fifty million orgasms and, mwahahaha, how perfect is that?*"

An old woman wrapped in a flowered shawl on her way to the trash bin by the bus stop shoots a judgmental look my way.

"He's awful. And British," I tell her.

Her gaze cuts to him then back to me, and then she nods in solidarity.

See? She gets it!

But I should also probably stop screaming about cocks on the street corner.

Releasing my ire for a nanosecond, I say more gently, "You didn't say a word when I told you the name of my business. The *name*, West."

"Like I said, Gigi, I can explain," he says, sounding sincere.

But I won't be fooled.

No way. I don't have room in my life for this kind of treachery. This is why dating is a minefield. And West Territory is just as deadly as Parrot Man Land and all the rest.

I need to bolt. It hurts to listen to him. My chest aches, and I feel stupid.

So stupid.

I liked him. Dammit. One night, and I already liked the man.

I gird myself with my best tough-as-nails attitude.

Chin all the way up.

"I don't want your explanations," I call back. "And I no longer wish to spend my morning with you. I'm going to see my grandmother, a woman who appreciates pie and has never lied to anyone. Ever. In her entire life."

"I wasn't lying, love." He has the nerve to grin, like he can flirt his way out of this as easily as he flirted his way into my bed. But I am much more protective of my pie shop than I am my pussy. Hurt my pussy, and only I suffer. Hurt my shop, and you endanger my entire family legacy.

"Let's go back to your place," he says. "Talk this out."

"I'll be back in a couple of hours. Please be gone by then," I say. "And don't bother texting. I won't read them."

And with that, I spin on my heel and head for the subway entrance on the other side of the traffic circle. He calls after me, something about "not being ridiculous" that only stiffens my resolve.

I am *not* ridiculous! I'm in charge of my family's business. I'm in control of the entire kit and caboodle. Everything is riding on me, and I can't afford to make mistakes right now. I can't sleep with the enemy, even if he is the very best at both spanking *and* pulling hair.

Sob. Thank God I got extra pieces of pie so West could try a variety of flavors. A morning like this calls for Gram girl-talk *and* serious pie therapy.

* * *

Gram used to say pie may not cure heartbreak, but it certainly makes it easier to swallow.

Everything goes down better with a slice of Chocolate Dream.

And she's right.

I stab my fork into a slice, chew, then chase it with coffee.

Strong, black coffee that fuels me.

"Trying to poke a hole through Gram's good china?" my brother, Harrison, asks, arching a perfectly plucked brow at my pie plate.

I got a two-fer, since my brother is at Gram's house for their Sunday morning poker game. Gram already cleaned up—she was scooping fifty bucks in chips into her hot little hands when I swept into her Brooklyn townhouse in a cloud of righteous fury.

I wrap my arm lovingly around the dessert plate with the kitschy dancing chipmunk illustration. As Gram says—why eat on plates with vines when you can eat with dancing chipmunks?

"I would never wound such a beautiful thing. I *love* beautiful things. I *love* this plate and this sweet little fork. And I love you," I say to my brother, who accepts my love with an affectionate roll of his ice-blue eyes.

I turn to Gram, my growing-old-gracefully idol with her starburst smile lines and Helen Mirren grace, "And I love you." I inhale deeply, then gesture to the feline in her lap. "I love Joan too, even though she detests me."

"She detests everyone, sweetie pie. She's a cat."

"But I do not even *like* that man," I continue, "I mean, really. Who chooses to peddle tea when there's coffee to be had?"

"Tea lovers," Harrison offers, so deadpan he should deliver the weekend updates on Saturday Night Live.

"Gag." I dig into the pie, devouring another forkful before I add, "Tea lovers are the new men with parrots. But never fear. I have plans. Plans to hate him for all eternity. Mark my words."

Harrison's arched brow asks, *are you sure you can pull that off, little sis?* His brows have their own language, and I am fluent in it.

"Yes, I can pull it off," I answer.

He snorts. "And how exactly do you plan to do that, Miss I Love Everything and Want to Give the World A Hug? And a piece of pie?"

I huff. "I do not love everything." Though I admit he's right about the pie. There are people going hungry every day. They deserve pie. For sustenance and solace in their times of trial.

Gram chuckles as she strokes the gigantic cat's head, and Joan emits an appreciative purr, one that I believe translates as *I permit you three more strokes of my royal fur before I leap off you, retreat to a window, and fastidiously lick the spot you touched.* With her free hand, Gram scoops out a slice of grapefruit. "Says the girl who just expressed her love for plates and forks and everyone in this room, including the world's most people-hating cat."

"*That,*" I say, pointing to the offending citrus as exhibit A. "I do not love grapefruit. Especially with coffee. What are you doing to your tastebuds, woman?"

"I don't mind it," she offers mildly as she takes another spoonful. "And grapefruit is good for you."

"So is kale," I say. "And I definitely don't love *it*. Come to think of it, I hate it, along with beets and turnips. Also, I'm deeply opposed to pears. They taste like sand, they're the worst Christmas gift ever, and even *I* can't make them work in a pie without drowning them in caramel sauce."

Harrison removes his glasses and pinches the bridge of his nose, laughing. He raises his face, a smirk still playing on his lips. "Yes, I recall your third-grade presentation on the loathsomeness of pears. One of the few times I can remember you complaining about anything Mom put on the table." He takes a beat and locks eyes with me. "And that's my point."

"You're not a hater, sweetie pie," Gram agrees as she runs a hand down the cat's smoky head, and right on cue, the gorgeous beast leaps off her lap.

"But I am!" I press a fist to my chest. "I am full of righteous fury and indignation. Like Joan. Or maybe like Hellfire or Brimstone or whatever those comic book characters are. Ghost Rider? Something like that?"

Harrison lifts his hands in surrender. "Don't ask me. I don't read comics."

"Nor do I," Gram puts in. "If it didn't happen in a salacious celebrity memoir, I didn't read it. Speaking of, did you hear that when Patti LuPone was fired from *Sunset Boulevard*, she trashed her dressing room? Smashed her lamp *and* her mirror," Gram says, sounding enjoyably scandalized by the Tony winner's rage. "That woman has some serious chutzpah."

"Idea." Harrison sits up straighter. "You could name a pie after her during the Mrs. Sweet Stuff competition. Call it the Seriously Sweet Chutzpah, and be sure to use caramel for the sweet and something salted for the serious bit. But no pears."

Harrison is great with plays on words for pies. He's a book editor at Bailey and Brooks Publishing and has nabbed some big titles in recent years.

"It could work," I say, shoveling in more pie. "Though I confess I'm not a huge fan of the diva thing. I keep thinking of all the poor people who have to clean up the mess after a famous person throws a fit."

"And you prove my point again," Harrison says. "You've hated three things in your life." He counts them off on his fingers. "The aforementioned food items, bad fashion–"

"Well, bad fashion is unacceptable," I sputter.

"And spiders," he continues.

Gram chuckles and takes another bite of her sub-par citrus snack.

"What's so funny?" I ask.

"You don't even hate spiders," she says with a knowing grin. "Not really. Whenever you found one in your room, you'd ask Grandpa to catch it in a jar and put it outside."

"Because I'm not a killer."

"Our point, exactly," Gram says. "You're a sweet soul to the bone, pumpkin. I don't see you managing to hate this man for all eternity, especially since he actually sounds… Well, rather delightful."

My jaw drops. "You're siding with the enemy?"

Harrison whips out his phone. "His name is West? His shop is Tea and Empathy?"

I scowl. "Yes."

Ten seconds later, my brother swivels the phone around, revealing a smiling photo of West and a tiny sprite who has his nose and elegant brow in feminine miniature. His sister? "Weston Byron. Hmmm… I don't know, G. If a man that hot took me home and tossed me up against—"

I shoot him a *do not go to dirty land in front of Gram* nostril flare and mime zipping my lips.

Gram rolls her eyes. "As if I don't know how that works. Proceed."

Harrison leans back in his chair. "All I'm saying is if a man like that took me out for drinks and beguiled me with his wit and sensual prowess, and then the next morning said he wanted to explain why he hadn't mentioned he worked at Lerner and Lowe Publishing..." He pauses to pin me with his stare. "I'd listen to every word then say *fine, handsome, let's go get a sandwich*."

Gram pats his hand. "You always were a good listener, Harrison."

I whip my gaze to her. "Gram! This is a big deal! This is a betrayal. He tricked me."

"Gigi, think about it. What sort of person is so nefarious that he scouts out the baker across the street, follows her to an obscure party, where he just happens to share her odd, niche interests—"

I start to insist that Rubik's Cube isn't all that niche, or odd, but she presses on.

"Then treats her to drinks and wonderful conversation, and ends the night with generous, mutually enjoyable sex? Just to scope out the competition? Isn't that a little...elaborate? And how common is sweet shoppe espionage, really?"

I start to protest, but that's the thing about Gram—she's always been my moral compass. She has a keen sense of people and what makes them tick. She's calm, thoughtful, and exceedingly rational.

"It sounds like—*perhaps*—he was so enchanted by you that he wanted to enjoy your wit and charm and save the shoptalk for later. Consider that?" she asks gently.

Rationally.

Calmly.

And that does sound…nice.

"What's the worst thing that could happen if you give him another chance?" Harrison chimes in, then silently mouths, *More orgasms?*

Hmmm…would that be the worst?

Or the best?

Annoyance slithers through me for a few more minutes, but once my coffee cup is drained, my frustration has vanished too.

Maybe I did overreact. Maybe I assumed the worst without just cause. Maybe the last few years of dating The Bachelors from the Weirdo Lagoon has colored my world view.

Might I have given up on West too soon?

"You're right," I grumble. "I should talk to him. At least give him a chance to explain."

"Excellent choice," Gram says.

Harrison taps my cell phone on the table beside my empty cup. "Do it now. Send him a text before he thinks you're cray cray."

"Which he very well might," Gram adds.

They may have a point.

The longer I think on it, the more sweet shoppe espionage does seem a little out there.

I grab my phone, about to tap out an olive branch message when I spot another email from the competition organizers.

The subject line reads *Good News, Contestants.*

Yay! Good news! This email is clearly a sign. I'm being calm and thoughtful, and the universe is rewarding me.

I take a moment to practice my ritual—reminding myself of the lovely things in life. I have great friends and the best family in the world, so much so that it hardly matters that I'm not close to my parents.

And I have Sweetie Pies, and my darling and I have a lot to accomplish together.

Maybe, just maybe, I can have it all—including another date with West.

"Fine, West is probably not kale," I say to my brother as Gram takes the plates to the kitchen. "He's more like a whiskey sweet potato pie with cinnamon and nutmeg."

"Yum. Find out if West has a brother who likes poker and exceptionally good-looking book editors."

"I'll make no such inquiry," I say with a smile as I swipe open the email and begin to read. "But I will text him, right after I—"

I break off with a gasp and drop my phone like it's hot.

I see red—fire engine red as smoke billows from my eyes.

"What is it?" Harrison asks, concerned. "Did the

promo code I sent for fifty percent off at Twice Around expire before you could use it?"

"Worse! West *is* out to get me." I tap a frantic nail on the phone. "He's in the competition! West Byron is in the Mr. or Mrs. Sweet Stuff contest. His name is right under mine!" I shove the screen in my brother's face. His eyes widen, confirming that this is bad news. Very bad indeed. "That's it. No second chances," I hiss. "This man is my nemesis. I *will* despise him for all eternity. Even if I'm not very good at it at first."

Surely, there must be a guidebook somewhere. A do-it-yourself handbook on how to detest a man who gave you a quartet of Os.

* * *

Once I leave Gram's place, waving goodbye to Joan, who thoroughly ignores me, as cats do, I text Rosie, my writer friend, on my way to the subway.

Gigi: Idea for a new short story. Man gives a woman four Os. Next day, she learns he's her nemesis. What happens next?

Rosie: Ooh, great question. In this choose-your-own-adventure tale, I say she bangs him again because hate-sex is hot.

Ugh. Rosie's no help.
There will be *no* banging. No hate-sex.

But then, how hot would hate-sex with West be? Probably super-duper hot, with lots of spanking and—

Nope. Stop it. Bad, Gigi.

But as I march down the steps to the subway, I can't help lingering on hot hate-sex for a second.

I swear, only for a second.

Fine, maybe a minute. Or twelve.

8

WEST

Seeing as Gigi made it clear she isn't in the mood for further conversation—at least *with me*—I decide against chasing her across the park to kiss her until she realizes I'm not a tea-peddling monster out to steal her business.

At least, I suppose that's what she's upset about.

There's room in the world for more than one sweet shoppe per block, and I highly doubt a customer can get a decent cup of tea at her place. And many of us enjoy a fine, smoky, sweet tea with dessert.

So, I'm not competing with her so much as complementing her.

Once she cools off, I'll be able to make her realize that. Until the text explosion, she seemed like a sensible woman. She's certainly the sexiest woman in New York —potentially in the entire Northern Hemisphere—and I refuse to let a silly misunderstanding keep me from making her come on my cock at least a dozen more times.

This week, in fact.

Deciding to pave the way to fucking and making up, I assemble an "I'm sorry I didn't tell you I'm opening a store across the street from yours" present from the items on my shelves. Because, she did have a point. Perhaps I was a bit cagey when I learned about her shop. I should have told her about mine then, if not earlier in the night. She has me there.

Hence, the apology gift—a cedar box filled with premium tea samples, a blue and yellow ceramic teapot that will fit right in with her colorful décor, and some lavender and honey candies that pair perfectly with my signature blend of Earl Grey. Who doesn't love Earl Grey?

I type out a quick note asking for a chance to explain myself properly, tuck it into the box, and start for the door, only to think twice and pop into the back room for more supplies.

Over at her apartment, I arrange my offering on her kitchen counter, leave the key on the hook, and pull the locked door closed behind me.

I'm about to head home when a familiar voice calls my name. "West! Over here!"

My little sister, Abby, is standing in front of the shop across the street. Actually, she's waving her arm over her head and jumping up and down in front of the shop, grinning so wide I can spot her twin dimples from here.

I've seen Abby nearly every day for the last six months, but I haven't seen her dimples in all that time. Not since her evil ex, Hawley, broke off their engagement via text message and then refused to return her phone calls begging him to explain what happened.

He just tossed the "it's over" bomb through the window and then dropped off the face of the earth.

Miserable wanker.

I fully intend to punch him in the spleen if our paths ever cross again. No one destroys my sister's heart and her self-esteem and gets away with it. I'd begun to think he'd stolen her smile too, but there it is, bright and shiny as ever.

I can't help but smile too, even though my cock is still busy fretting that we might never see Gigi again. He's confident in his abilities, but he's also a greedy bastard who can't get enough of a good thing.

And Gigi is definitely a good thing.

"Good morning, cheery face," I say, opening an arm to Abby as I step up on the sidewalk beside her.

My very *little* little sis—she's barely five feet tall in sneakers—bounds in for a hug even more enthusiastic than I'm expecting, squeezing me so tight I grunt, proving she's small but fierce. "Oh my God, it's the best morning, West. The very best! Look!" She pulls back and shoves her cell into my face.

I rear back, blinking, and laugh. "Too close. Jesus, my eyes. What am I even looking at?"

"You made it!" she says, bouncing up and down, making it even more difficult to read her screen. "You're in the running to become this year's Mr. Sweet Stuff!"

The phrase sounds vaguely familiar, but I can't resist teasing her. "Is that a sex thing? If so, I'm definitely more salty than sweet."

"No." She slaps my arm affectionately and rolls her brown eyes. "It's the Brooklyn Mr. or Mrs. Sweet Stuff competition." She sighs when my expression remains blank. "Big time baking competition? Winner gets bragging rights and tons of free promo for their business for an entire year? Been going on for fifty years? Super prestigious? Any of this ringing a bell?"

"Um…" I wrinkle my nose.

She slaps me again, with less affection this time. "I told you about it months ago, when we first started working on the shop, but you said you didn't want to enter because we wouldn't be open in time. But I knew we would, so I entered you anyway." She lifts her phone again, beaming. "And you're in! Look!"

I take the phone, skimming the email, a prickle of foreboding lifting the hairs at the back of my neck.

Five names down on the list of contestants, I realize why, and curse. "I can't, Abby," I say, nodding toward the phone. "I slept with contestant number five last night."

Her jaw drops. "What? You didn't."

"I did," I confirm. "And I want to keep sleeping with her more than I want to be the candy king of New York, so…" I try to hand the phone back to her, but she holds up both hands, fingers spread wide.

"It's Mr. Sweet Stuff, and you don't get it, West," she says, shoving her dark curls off her forehead. "This is a *huge* deal. They only pick ten bakers from thousands who apply. Just competing is all we need to ensure an amazing launch for the shop. And if you win, we're virtually guaranteed to be in the black by Christmas."

I hesitate. Being in the black isn't my primary goal—I know food service isn't a high-return endeavor, and I have enough money to operate at a loss for the rest of my life if I want to—but a successful launch would be a good thing.

And not just for our pocketbooks. The shop is much more than that.

Abby and I have planned to open a tea shop featuring our mother's recipes since I was eighteen and she was fifteen. We grew up cooking with our mum. While our older brothers were killing each other at rugby, Abby and I spent our afternoons in the kitchen, whipping up treats and playing board games while we waited for them to cook. After Mum lost her fight with breast cancer, we helped each other heal by imagining how, one day, we'd share her cooking with the world. Brooklyn seemed a perfect place to start.

It doesn't matter that Abby's a horrid chef. This has been her dream as much as mine, but unlike me, she only has a small nest egg. She didn't follow the Byron family rules. She dropped out of her banking program at university to get a degree in early childhood education and taught primary school before moving to the states. She won't have money to burn until my father passes and she receives her inheritance—which will hopefully be far in the future, seeing as we both enjoy our father quite a bit, even if he is a numbers guy and actively dislikes anything with sugar in it.

This competition could ensure Abby's financial success *and* bringing attention to Mum's amazing food.

I'm already wavering when Abby stabs a finger at the phone screen. "And you haven't seen the best part yet. Winning comes with a side of vengeance."

Frowning, I glance down to see the name of the tenth and final contestant—Frederick James Ebenezer Hawley.

Or "Hawley" for short.

Did I mention my sis's fucking wanker of a former fiancé is also a world-famous pastry chef with his own line of gourmet frozen treats? And that, after he cheated on her and dumped her, he bragged that his eclairs were better than our scones?

Any man who would treat my sweet Abby with so little care *and* disparage our family recipes deserves to be defeated on the field of battle.

Humiliatingly defeated.

And I'm just the man to deliver that trouncing, with a side of fist in the spleen.

That also means my apology to Gigi might require a bit more finesse. I need to make sure she understands that I wasn't tricking her with my perfect cock.

Though, I like that she's put it on a cock pedestal.

Perhaps, a swim in the gym pool will clear my head. I'll swim, work on recipes with Abby, and then spend the evening planning exactly what to say to my pie shop beauty.

Tomorrow, I'll be ready.

9

GIGI

So sorry. Please let me explain.

The words are spelled out in Scrabble letters on my kitchen counter in front of a lovely—and disgustingly tea-centric—present. But the tea pot is so adorable and so *me* that it almost makes me wish I liked tea.

"But I don't," I say, tucking the gift and the tiles behind the toaster oven so I don't have to deal with them right now. And so that Ruby—who just buzzed downstairs—can't see them.

I meet my cousin at the door, cooing with excitement when I see what she's carrying, "Oh my goodness, what is this? For me?"

"Of course!" Ruby hands over the most adorable bouquet of brightly colored lollipops, tied up with a big red bow. "It's a congratulations on winning Mrs. Sweets present!"

"Stop," I say, laughing as she hugs me tight. "Don't jinx me. The competition's stiff this year."

"So I heard," she says, bobbing her brows up and

down. "So, you slept with the enemy, huh? You really do have the worst luck with men, babes."

"Ugh, I know. Nelson, Theodore, Shelby..." I rattle off my trio of horrible exes as I roll my eyes. "I assume Harrison called you?"

"He's concerned. Thought you might need help destressing about Sexy Yet Traitorous Tea Guy before things get started tomorrow."

I shake my head, forcing an easy smile. "Nope. Everything's fine. I'm totally focused and ready to bring my A game. You know me, I don't get distracted by boys."

She narrows her brown eyes, studying me closely, but apparently my poker face is strong this evening. "Okay. This means we're free to focus on picking out the most amazing outfit ever, right?"

I clap my hands and squeal, "Yes! I'm so glad you're here. You can order Chinese, while I put on a fashion show. I'm going to try on everything in my closet. Twice."

Ruby grins. "Perfect. Though, I will have to head back to my place by seven to meet Jesse. And I *will* want to hear all about this awful, yet incredible-in-bed, Englishman at some point. After you beat him and talking about him doesn't stress you out anymore, of course."

"I'm not stressed," I repeat in a breezy voice. "But that sounds perfect. I'll be turning in early tonight, anyway. Beauty sleep, you know."

But many hours later—after Ruby and I have laughed and eaten Chinese and picked out the world's most perfect dress for tomorrow—I lie in bed with my thoughts spinning and Scrabble tiles dancing in my head.

Tiles that keep rearranging themselves to spell Weston Byron's name.

* * *

The next day, Sweetie Pies is a madhouse.

Summers are usually a little slower for us than the rest of the year, when thoughts naturally turn to pies, sweet indulgences, and family celebrations. But for some reason this morning everyone and their bossy grandmother who's allergic to cinnamon and hates raisins is lined up at my counter, loudly demanding to know the daily specials even though there's a giant chalkboard detailing them in ten-inch letters right behind my head.

I adore my customers, but by eleven, my customer service face has gotten quite the work out, and I'm secretly relieved for an excuse to cut out early to get showered and spiffed up for the first round of the competition.

It doesn't start until three and I'm only a ten-minute walk from the location—the first round is always held in a big, beautiful tent in Prospect Park with a view of the lake—but I'm hoping to grab a power nap too. I slept poorly, plagued by dreams of a handsome, yet dastardly Brit.

Mr. Weston Byron was swaggering through my head all night, so I'm not surprised when he swaggers through the front door of my shop right as I'm ducking under the counter to head home.

Still, the sight of him stops me dead in my tracks.

Dead. Like I've been zapped by a freeze ray.

For a second I think it's his eyes, those penetrate-me-five-different-ways eyes that instantly make my panties damp.

But then I realize what's shocked me and blurt out, "Your beard."

His hand drifts to his newly bare face with a cautious smile. "Yeah. I thought I should clean up a bit. For the um…cameras and all."

The cameras. Right. Must not forget he's a traitor. A dirty, lying, sex-tricking traitor.

I stand up straight and lift my chin, shaking off the stunning effects of his man beauty. "Of course. You look very nice without a beard."

"Thank you," he says, shifting to one side as two familiar little girls with a takeout bag dash out the door, racing each other to their push scooters. "I was hoping—"

"Just a second." I hurry past him, sticking my head out the open door to shout, "Be careful, Emily! Jane! If you bring home broken pie crust again, your moms won't let you do the pick-up. And you know I need girl talk. How else am I going to keep up with the gossip?"

Emily instantly slows, reaching out to snag Jane by the elbow. They both turn back to me with big grins.

"We'll be careful!" Jane calls. "We promise."

"And we'll hook you up next week," Emily says, propping a dramatic hand on her hip "So much is happening right now you can't miss an update or you will be *so* lost, girl."

"Good. Scoot safe." I wave goodbye with a grin that fades as I turn back to West and sniff. "Yes?"

He glances out the window at the girls then back at me. "You're good with kids, I see?"

I frown. "No, I'm good with people. Kids are people. Less annoying, smaller people who need grown-ups to listen to them more often. Especially when they're twelve. Twelve is hard."

"I agree," he says. "My sister had a rough time around that age. She was so much smaller than the other girls that they treated her like an annoying infant. Wouldn't let her join in all the pre-teen girl reindeer games, tortured her with awful nicknames, put dirty nappies in her purse, etcetera."

I wince. "I'm sorry. That's awful. My brother was one of the first people in his class to come out in high school. Some of the tough guys made his life a living hell."

West's brow furrows as he nods. "My oldest brother, Pierce, is gay. Got into a few fights at uni, when the footballers didn't care to see him and his boyfriend holding hands."

"Yeah. Harrison used to get jumped too." I'm glad my brother's grown up and no one puts hate notes in his locker anymore—and silently intrigued that West *does* have a brother who might like a handsome book editor. "But he turned out all the more fabulous for the hard times. He's both one of the strongest and kindest people I know."

"Same with Pierce, though he's a heartless invest-ment banker from nine to five. But Abby...she's all sweetness." He pulls in a breath, seeming to brace himself as he adds, "The kind of sweet that believes in her brother enough to enter him into a prestigious dessert competition without his knowledge."

I arch a dubious brow. "Is that so?"

"It is. If I'd told you sooner that I was opening up across the street it would probably be easier to believe, but..."

"Why *didn't* you tell me?" I ask, wishing we'd taken this outside for privacy. I don't have to turn around to know my staff is hanging on every word. With only a few customers in the shop, my crew would normally be chatting and swapping fashion tips while they tidy up. Instead, the counter area is dead silent.

I lift a hand before West can reply. "Actually, let's take this to the sidewalk, shall we?"

"So you can rough me up if you don't like my answer?"

"Yes." I hate the flirty note in my voice, but I can't seem to help it. I'm so irritated with this man, but still his sparkly eyes and easy way with words captivate me.

And his forearms are *really* pretty in that cranberry button-up with the sleeves rolled back. Yum, yum, yum.

Discreetly wiping the drool from the corner of my mouth, I flutter my fingers at my counter staff, fighting a smile at their faces, looking so indignant that I'm depriving the three of them of juicy gossip.

Just as well. They'll only be disappointed when they realize my handsome new beau is the enemy in disguise.

At least, I'm pretty sure he's still on my shit list. But that gift *was* quite nice, tea aside. Plus, there's how he went to the trouble of spelling out *So sorry*.

I should let him explain himself. If there's a fairy godmother raining down Hot British Men on sex-starved American women, I don't want to miss out. I'll take her blessing in the form of a kiss to discover how his clean-shaven jaw feels against my face.

Just for research, and all.

"So? Talk," I order, as we wander down the sidewalk toward my place. "Why were you so shady the other night?"

"I didn't mean to be shady. When we arrived at yours, I was focused on more interesting things than talking about my shop. Once you told me you own Sweetie Pies, I would have come clean, but I became distracted again. But I would have told you. I promise."

I narrow my eyes. "Huh."

He raises his right hand. "I swear on my sister's life. I went to fetch some tea to have with our pie, planning to tell you as soon as we sat down for breakfast."

I wrinkle my nose. "I don't like tea though I appreciate your gift."

His brows shoot up. "What? You don't like tea?"

"I don't like it. Sorry. It's just not to my taste."

"But you'll guzzle rancid motor oil all night?" he asks, amused but judgy. "Without even any cream or sugar in it to soften the blow?"

"I love coffee. Don't talk about it that way, you'll hurt its feelings."

He snorts. "It's too bitter to have feelings."

"At least it doesn't taste like wet crabgrass."

"Wet crabgrass?"

"Yes, and not even wet from the rain. Wet because a dog peed on it. A poorly hydrated dog who needs to go to the vet to get checked out because it might have a bladder infection."

His newly beard-free cheeks stretch into a grin, revealing a dimple on his right side.

A dimple! God, I love dimples. I want to press my finger into it to mark the spot and then kiss it.

"Darling, I think you might be drinking the wrong tea. Or eating the wrong chocolate. Have you ever had an Earl Grey chocolate bar?"

I nearly retch. "Why would I do that to chocolate?"

He tosses his head back and laughs. "Why *wouldn't* you is the better question. Earl Grey is one of the few things that can make chocolate even better. Someday I will bring you one of the finest Earl Grey chocolate bars." He takes a beat to let his gaze hold mine. "It's my favorite. I'm helpless before it."

He's talking about chocolate, but it feels like he's talking about me. The way he stares. The way his eyes linger on my face.

My chest swoops.

And, once again, temptation strikes.

The desire to kiss this man is powerful, but I find the will to resist.

I stop in front of my apartment and turn to Weston, the gorgeous and potentially-not-evil owner of the shop across the street. "So, you didn't plan to lure me in with sex and then commit heinous acts of corporate espionage? I mean, you *are* the competition. And I'm not just talking about the Mr. or Mrs. Sweet thing. Your shop is literally right across the street, primed to siphon away my business."

He looks stunned, as if no such thought has ever crossed his mind. "I honestly never thought about it that way."

"What way did you think about it?" I ask, legitimately curious. "You saw a well-established dessert shop already here and decided to open another one?"

He shakes his head. "Nothing really. There are cupcake shops and ice cream parlors all over the neighborhood. They all seem to be doing well. I suppose I figured there was enough room for a pie shop and a cozy nook for tea, scones, and finger sandwiches. But truly, it wasn't something that concerned me. For good or ill, it never entered my mind."

I sigh, nibble my bottom lip, and sigh again.

West cocks his head and lifts an expressive brow my brother would envy. It's a brow that says, "can we be friends now?"

And I guess friends seems the way to go.

"Yes," I say to the most-likely-*not*-evil West. But sadly, that doesn't change things for us. Our businesses might end up harmoniously co-existing, but we're still adversaries.

I know myself. Another date, another time with him, and I'll lose sight of my priorities. Sweetie Pies is my focus. The Mrs. Sweets competition is my big goal. Anything else with this man will distract me.

"Yes, you believe me?" he asks.

"I believe you, but I don't think we should keep that lunch date. Not when we're going to be pitted against each other in the heat of battle."

He grins that charming, sexy grin of his. "I don't know. We faced each other on the field of battle the other night and ended up getting along just fine."

"Scrabble is different," I say. "Scrabble is a game. This is business. Serious business. I assume you agree, or you would have dropped out of the contest by now."

He sobers. "It's important to my sister that I compete. And, upon closer thought important to me too."

"I completely understand," I say, pain flashing in my chest. I *do* understand, but that doesn't mean I have to like being forced to turn my back on the first guy to make me feel beautiful and desirable in so long.

But this is part of being a business owner who puts her work family's needs first.

I stick out a hand. "May the best baker win."

His fingers curl around mine and squeeze, sending longing dancing across my skin. And then he pulls me into him, and my breath rushes out as my breasts collide with his chest.

I start to pull away, but I don't want to. I want to give in. I want to be kissed again. I want to know if his beardless kisses are as delish as his bearded ones.

Then, his hand is cradling my head, and his lips are on mine, and he's kissing me the way he kisses me—like I'm delicious and delightful. Like I'm the last bite of warm raspberry trifle smothered in melting ice cream and he's determined to savor every little scrap of me.

His tongue teases against mine, then strokes, making my breath come faster and my arms twine around his neck like vines seeking the steadiness of a sturdy stake to climb.

And yes, I want to climb him. I want to jump into his arms, wrap my legs around his hips, and order him to my bed, posthaste.

Clean-shaven West kisses as spectacularly as bearded West.

But that's the problem.

I could drown in these kisses. I'm not a hater, I'm a lover, and having a lover like him will turn my brain to pear mush.

He pulls away and presses a kiss to my forehead. "Just a goodbye kiss. For good luck," he says in a husky voice.

Damn. His voice melts me too.

Yes, it's best I didn't issue any ill-advised invitations to take him to bed. I need to rest and focus, not get lost in West's kisses.

"Right." My breath shudders out as I force myself to take a step back. I look up at him and nod. "Goodbye, then. And good luck."

"Smashing good luck. I can't wait to see you perform under pressure. I have no doubt you'll be brilliant."

My lips part, then close, then part. I'm struggling to sort out a response to such sweetness from an adversary, when West adds with a sigh, "But fair warning, I'm still probably going to beat you. I'm very good at what I do. *Everything* I do."

Crossing my arms, I shoot him my best cat-who-shredded-the-dog's-favorite-squeaky-toy grin. "As am I, sir… As am I."

He matches my evil grin and raises me a wink. "You certainly are, Ms. James. This is going to be fun."

As I watch him walk away, heading back toward the park, I shake my head.

Fun isn't the word I would use, but it's certainly going to be…something.

10

WEST

That kiss was a bad idea.

A *really* bad idea.

I'm not usually the sort of bloke who has trouble staying on task. But as I check in with the contest coordinator at the festive Mr. or Mrs. Sweet Stuff tent in Prospect Park a few hours later, I struggle to concentrate as the woman leads me to my cooking station, explaining my setup. I keep scanning the space for a sign of Gigi. Will her station be near mine?

I keep thinking about that kiss too, and how much I want another one. And another. That woman's mouth has exposed a gluttonous side of my personality I wasn't aware existed before we met.

I'm not sure I like it.

"Weston, old boy," a deep, wanker-ish voice shouts.

I curse under my breath. This is the problem with Gigi. She's so damn distracting that I didn't spot Hawley the Wretched before he saw me.

I turn to see the loathsome pastry chef waving from the cooking station behind mine.

"What are the chances?" he asks, grinning. "Two old school friends locking horns half a world away. I hope you'll let me take you out for a pint after we finish up today. I'd love to talk, hash things out, get back to being mates again."

I let my cool gaze skim him up and down.

He's impeccably dressed, as usual. His pink-and-blue plaid summer suit should look ridiculous, but he somehow manages to pull it off with aplomb. Hawley is an arrogant arse, but he's a good-looking man, by all accounts, who knows how to put himself together. And he can be charming when he wants to be.

I can't fault my sister for falling for him. And Hawley certainly did seem devoted to her while they were together. He fooled even me there.

But I won't forgive what he did to my sister, and I certainly know better than to let my guard down around this two-faced, back-stabbing goblin.

I turn away without a response, deciding the Cut Direct is the best response in this situation. In Regency times, my Byron ancestors excelled at the art of staring straight in the face a friend who'd fallen out of favor, while pretending not to have a clue who he was.

I'm bringing it back, and it feels good to leave Hawley sputtering while I turn a kind smile on the petite Asian woman at the station across from mine. She has a slick page boy cut and red-framed glasses a bit too large for her small face, but there's a friendly light in her eyes. "Hello, I'm Weston. Nice to meet you."

"Willow," she whispers so softly I can barely hear her. "Good to meet you too." Her fingers flutter at her throat, tugging the top of her lacy shirt away from her neck. Cartoon cupcakes dance on her pink apron. "I'm so nervous."

"Don't be," I assure her. "I think a lot of us are new to the competition scene. We'll stumble along together."

Her cheeks flush. "Thank you. I just hope the judges don't yell like that angry chef on TV."

"I doubt it. All the people I've met so far have been quite nice," I say, then add in a confidential voice, "And the grouchy chef? He's a friend of the family and a total lamb off-screen. The going-mental thing is mostly an act for the cameras."

"Really?" Her hand drops to the counter of her station, and she seems to relax a little.

"Really. And no one's going to be worried about ratings here, so we should be safe from unnecessary drama."

She nods and tucks her hair shyly behind one ear but doesn't make any further attempt at conversation. Which is probably good since, at that moment, Gigi steps into the tent, following the same woman who guided me down the center aisle between the stations. The stunning redhead is wearing a dress that drops my jaw to the floor.

Glossy red fabric wraps around her neck, criss-crossing at her breasts and nipping in at her waist before flaring into a poof around her legs. The dress is…blisteringly hot, but it's the fluffy black underskirt beneath it that has my fingers itching and my cock thickening behind the fly of my black suit pants.

I pushed a very similar fluffy skirt up her thighs just two nights ago. Memories of the way it bunched around her waist as I devoured her sweet, hot pussy flood my head as she swishes by, shooting me a sultry glance from the corner of her eyes that nearly knocks me off my feet.

"Stop it," I hiss as she passes.

She laughs under her breath but doesn't respond. She's listening to the woman explaining that the small ovens we're using tend to run a few degrees hot and that there's a chance she'll blow a fuse if she runs more than two or three appliances at a time.

Hm. Good to know.

I make a mental note to turn off the mixer for the scone batter before I start whipping my lemon-infused cream. My English take on the "Classic New York Dessert" we're creating for this first challenge—lemon-strawberry shortcake served on toasted scones with cream and shortbread crumble—is fairly simple, but I will have several ingredients going at the same time.

I jot a reminder on my notepad and then go back to admiring Gigi's ensemble. And I'm not the only one. Wretched Hawley is slobbering on his shirt as he crosses to introduce himself, making me wish I'd warned Gigi that there was a sister-destroying monster in our midst.

But I needn't have worried. Gigi is pleasant, but distant, and sends him on his way after just a few moments. Hawley crosses behind the cooking stations, giving each one a thorough once over.

Move along, wanker. Move along.

He lingers near Willow's a few more seconds, bending over to tie his shoe or something, then marches on.

Once he's back in his station, Gigi turns to Willow and begins a warm conversation clearly designed to put the anxious creature at ease. I overhear bits and pieces.

"I stopped in your shop the other week. The cinnamon roll cupcake was genius."

"Oh, thank you. I've always loved cinnamon rolls and, well, of course I love cupcakes," Willow replies.

"And to marry them together?" Gigi gives a chef's kiss.

Willow's smile lights up her face. "And the cinnamon rolls and cupcakes lived happily ever after."

I smile too, at the Gigi Effect. Willow seems more relaxed after talking to her.

The redhead truly is an excellent judge of character. She shouldn't doubt herself. Or me. I'm wonderful, and as soon as this contest is over, I'll prove it to her.

Because I do need to kiss her again. Soon.

As if sensing the direction of my thoughts, she shifts her attention my way, her lips curving in a wry smile as she shakes her head. "It won't work," she calls out. "I refuse to be distracted by…any of that."

"I have no idea what you're talking about," I say with a grin, pleased that she finds me as distracting as I find her.

"Welcome contestants! And welcome, Brooklyn!"

The short, pudgy man with the thick gray beard who seems to be running the competition waves to us from a small stage at the front of the tent. Behind him, several hundred people have gathered.

People who cheer as he turns to wave their way.

They're so loud Willow flinches and looks ready to dive under her counter to hide. And I confess, my own pulse picks up a little. I didn't expect this to be so public. Or performative.

But as the cheering crowd is allowed past the entrance ropes to surround the tent—settling into lawn chairs they've brought with them or onto blankets spread on the grass—it's clear we're going to have an audience.

"Gigi! Gigi! Over here!" The call comes from behind me, and I turn to see a group of women—all ages and colors, with seemingly nothing in common but the big smiles on their faces—waving her way.

"Give 'em hell, kiddo!" an older woman wearing an unusually sexy pair of overalls shouts out. The woman beside her with the wild blond curls and killer smile seconds the sentiment.

"You're already our winner," says a younger woman with luminous dark brown skin and a stunning, big-eyed baby strapped to her chest with a shawl. Beside her, a pretty woman with brown hair and a heart-shaped face that reminds me a little of Gigi's shouts, "You're the goddess of pie, and don't you forget it."

I glance back at Gigi to see her blushing and shushing them, but it's clear she's happy to see her fan club.

I am too. She absolutely deserves a fan club.

Still, it makes me a little sad that I forbade Abby from coming. I didn't want her to be forced into close proximity with Wretched Hawley or to worry about how she's handling being near her ex for the first time since their split.

But now's not the time for emotions.

Now is the time for cooking.

I roll up my sleeves and get to work.

Thank you, mum, for the inspiration.

* * *

Forty minutes later, I put the finishing touches on the strawberry shortcake.

It smells fantastic and looks pretty enough for a centerfold shot in *Bon Appétit* magazine.

The scones and shortbread cookies, of course, I've made countless times, but the lemon infused cream was a new adventure—and a tricky one. If you don't get the measurements exactly right, the lemon will curdle the cream instead of leaving it delightfully zested.

But my cream is fucking gorgeous, perched like a cloud atop my perfect strawberry filling—not too liquid, not too dry.

I'm about to whip out my phone to document my beauty for the shop's social media when Gigi shrieks, "Willow! Fire! You're on fire!"

I whip my gaze to the right.

Oh, bloody hell.

Flame dances up the strings on Willow's apron. A ridiculously fast-moving flame.

"Oh." The tiny woman's eyes go wide, but she doesn't move to extinguish the flames. She simply presses both hands to her face and shouts, "Oh, no," in a slightly louder voice.

Instinct kicks in, replacing panic. There's no room for anything but swift, efficient action.

I drop my phone on my counter, grab a damp towel, and rush to Willow's station, arriving just as Gigi slides over the top of her counter to land beside the frozen woman.

She has a wet towel in hand, as well.

Fucking sexy as hell, I think as Gigi reaches for Willow's thigh, covering it with her towel. I do the same, joining in, and we smother the fire together.

A few seconds later, the fire is out, leaving behind nothing but the acrid smell of singed cotton.

"Oh my God, oh my God!" Willow hyperventilates as the last of the smoke wafts from her apron.

Gigi rests a hand on her shoulder and guides her to a stool at the rear of the station, closer to the onlookers on the grass, who are now applauding our rescue.

I wave in acknowledgment then crouch on one side of the stool as Gigi cradles Willow's hand on the other.

"Breathe, sweetie pie," Gigi says, petting her trembling fingers. "Just breathe."

Willow nods, gulping. I glance around for a cup, but don't see one. I do spot a water bottle sticking out of Willow's purse beneath the counter, however, and fill it at the sink.

"Thank you." She accepts the bottle and takes a small sip. "I'm so embarrassed."

"Nonsense. Fires happen in kitchens all the time," I reassure her. "Especially when you're in an unfamiliar space."

"Just a few weeks ago, I burned water," Gigi offers.

"Water?" Willow asks, confused.

"Yes. On the stove. My wooden spoon handle caught fire while I was boiling water for pasta," she says, then whispers. "But I was listening to Lady Gaga and singing along so it was mostly her fault. Plus, it was a good excuse to order out."

Willow laughs, and Gigi squeezes her knee.

My heart does an odd sort of gymnastics in my chest.

Strange, that.

"Thank you," Willow says to Gigi, then turns to me. "And you."

"Anytime," I say.

As we return to our stations to put the final touches on our dishes for the judges, Gigi's eyes stay on mine. She mouths, *So you're a fireman too?*

I answer her with a wink.

Because I'd like nothing more than to put out Gigi's fire.

11

GIGI

I wait as patiently as I can, with perfect posture.

Good posture helps me deal with being judged.

I've always loved cooking, and adored baking even more than worshipping at fashion's fickle altar—sorry, fashion, you know I love you. But I'm not a big fan of being judged.

Especially in public.

Reading reviews of the shop online gives me a rash, and when I entered a recipe for consideration in the "Brooklyn's Best Eats" charity cookbook, I had to call Ruby over to open the email for me when it arrived. I knew I'd fall into the shame-pit if I was rejected without a friend around to hold my hand and tell me it wasn't a big deal and there would be other cookbooks.

I just like things to be perfect and can't help stressing out when someone thinks my best effort isn't worthy of at least four out of five stars.

Growing up, perfection was one of the few things that seemed to make my parents happy. They loved that

I got good grades, crafted exceptional macaroni artwork, and went out of my way to make special desserts for them on their birthdays. They never seemed happy with each other, so I worked to bring them joy in other ways. I was too young to be conscious of it at the time, but looking back, it's clear being the perfect daughter was my plan for keeping my family together.

Too bad it didn't work.

Or maybe not. My parents are happier now that they're divorced and I'm happier now that I know they're both deeply flawed people who probably shouldn't have had children. I know they love me in their way, but it's not really a way that feels like love very often.

Doesn't take a degree in psychology to know that's also probably part of the reason I'm sweating right now, silently willing the judging to wrap up as soon as possible.

No matter how grown up I am, or how much I know I'm loved by Gram and Harrison and my aunt and uncle and Ruby, having parents who don't really care for you all that much can make a girl a little sensitive to criticism.

Two different chefs have already tasted my mini apple pies topped with hand-churned cinnamon ice cream and a caramel drizzle. I couldn't think of anything more American—or New York, hello, Big Apple—than classic apple pie and my take on the recipe is unique, zesty, and packed with flavor. The addition of the ice cream and drizzle add another layer of pure decadent yumminess.

Until this moment, I'd been confident that I'd nailed the perfect offering for the first challenge, but now I'm starting to wonder if apple pie is too simple.

Too trite.

Too…apple flavored.

The final judge, the grouchy one with the goatee, takes another bite of the crust—just the crust—pauses, then nods.

He sets down the plate, scribbles in his notebook, then strides to Mr. Skips, the organizer of the competition and one of the sweetest men in the sweets business. He ran the best wedding cake bakery in Brooklyn until he retired a few years back, leaving the business to his grandson.

Too bad he's not a judge this year. He's good friends with Aunt Barb and a *huge* fan of pie. And me. When we were kids, he always brought Ruby and me kites when he came to pick up his Easter desserts, and he still pops into Sweetie Pies regularly.

Not that I'd want special treatment or anything, but at least I'd know at least one judge appreciates my medium.

Some people just *don't like* pie.

Those people are obviously crazy, but…

After a few seconds that stretch on for an angst-filled eternity, Mr. Skips whirls around, strokes his cute little gray beard and clears his throat. "Good news, Sweet Lovers! We're ready to announce the point tallies for the first round! As a reminder, the rules stipulate that the contestant with the most points at the conclusion of the last event wins."

He takes a deep breath.

Then a freaking pregnant pause.

We all hang on his words—all ten contestants and the couple hundred onlookers gathered around the edge of the tent. He finally exhales, rattling off the fifth-place winner with seven points out of ten, and then my name is next.

"Gigi James with eight points for her lovely apple pie."

I beam. I hoped to make the top three, but there are a lot of talented chefs here. I'll take fourth and 8 out of 10 and be proud of my performance, thank you very much!

"And in third place." Mr. Skips glances back to his notes again, and chuckles, "Or well, I guess tied for fourth? Tied for third?" He laughs again. "In any event, West Byron, also finishes with 8 points for his innovative and refreshing strawberry shortcake."

What the...?

I jerk my gaze to West, who's blinking too, seemingly equally surprised that we're tied.

But he doesn't seem upset, and shockingly I find I'm not either. His shortcake was stunning. I wanted to eat it up with a spoon.

Or pop a dollop of that cream on a certain part of him and lick it off.

Stop it. No unicorn peen thoughts allowed, especially not while still on the field of battle.

Forcing a just-friends smile, I wrench my gaze from West's as Mr. Skips finishes calling out the scores.

Willow takes second place with her funnel cake flavored cupcake with caramel apple icing—a triumph I hope will restore her confidence after the fire. And then, as much as I hate to see the smarmy pastry chef come out on top, I'm not surprised when Hawley nabs first place with nine points.

I saw his pastry—a chocolate cherry crème puff in the shape of a...wait for it... Big Apple. With cherry glaze running down its perfectly rounded shape and delicate dark chocolate shavings dusted across the plate like autumn leaves, it was stunning.

Still, I find it hard to admire the man, there's something slimy about him, no matter how well-groomed he or his crème puff appear to be.

As soon as we're dismissed, I make it a point to head in the opposite direction of Mr. Pastry, hurrying around the back of the tent to find Rosie, Ruby, and the rest of my girls.

"You did it! Third place!" Ruby enthuses, pulling me in for a hug.

"And only one point between you and that massive prick in plaid," Rosie says, making me laugh. Because, of course, Rosie can spot a prick a mile away.

"And tied with Mr. Yummy Shortcake." Allana bobs her dark brows as she pats Reggie, her sleeping baby boy's bottom. "If I weren't a happily married woman, I would totally let him split my scone."

"Right in half," Rosie agrees, shooting a heated look West's way.

I clear my throat. "Um. Gross. I do not want my scone split, thank you very much. I want to keep my scone intact, my head in the game, and make sure I beat him next time around."

I chat with the girls for a bit longer, then excuse myself to gather my things from my station and tidy up. As I load my purse with the spices I brought from home, Willow tiptoes over to tap a timid finger on my counter. "I'd like to take you out, if that's okay. You and Weston? To say thank you."

"Oh, you don't—" I'm about to say *have to*, but I stop myself and think about how I'd feel if the shoe was on the other foot. If Willow had kept *me* from catching fire, I'd absolutely want to take her out. The look in her eyes tells me she feels the same way.

That this matters to her.

"Yes," I say with a smile. "I'd love that. Want me to ask West for you?"

Willow and I have been casual acquaintances for years—since she opened The Cupcakery in Williamsburg, in fact—but she's still shy with me. I'm assuming West must have her completely spooked, but she surprises me.

"No, I'll do it," she says, her lips twitching up on one side. "He's really nice. Reminds me of my big brother."

Aw. That's sweet, though I confess I'm secretly relieved West doesn't remind me of *my* big brother.

I watch as Willow asks him to join us, and the gentle way he accepts the invitation, and a warm fullness spreads through my chest.

He's not an evil tea-peddling trickster human. He's

kind and funny and gracious and heroic, and when he turns to me with a smile—clearly happy to join Willow and me—it's all I can do not to jump into his arms and pepper his big, sweet, sexy face with kisses.

Instead, I hitch my bag over my shoulder and nod toward the top of the Park. The sun sinks near the horizon as evening sets in. "Should we walk up by the museum? Avoid the subway?"

Willow nods. "There's a great diner up there. Amazing curly fries."

Twenty minutes later, I'm sliding into a shiny red booth next to Willow while West settles across from us. We order burgers and extra curly fries and chat about Brooklyn, trading stories of our favorite quirky natives, from the unicyclist couple who go for romantic, one-wheeled jaunts every night to the woman who brings her pet duck to the park in a baby carriage so it can visit with the wild waterfowl.

Willow nibbles a fry, then says, "And now *this* is one of my favorite stories about Brooklyn. I'm so grateful to the two of you." She takes a shaky breath. "That could have gone…really badly."

"Our pleasure," I say with a wave of my hand. "Don't think twice about it. Wasn't a big deal at all."

"But it was. You took time away from your dishes to help me, and I appreciate your kindness so much."

Something in her voice makes me think she's not used to kindness from strangers. Which is sad. Kindness is one of my favorite things.

"Well, I appreciate your cupcakes." I squeeze her hand then shift my attention to West. "You simply *must* try the cinnamon roll cupcakes at her shop. They're the best."

He seems delighted, his lips crooking into a grin. "Are they now? I'm a big fan of cinnamon."

My stomach rumbles with the memory, and I hum happily. "Then you'll love them. Absolutely delish. But she only makes them on weekends, so keep that in mind."

"Or let me know ahead of time that you're coming," Willow says with a smile. "I can make some special. We chefs have to stick together, right?"

"Except Hawley." West's smile vanishes as clouds sweep in behind his eyes. "Don't turn your back on that one. Especially if there are any knives around. You'll end up with one right between the shoulder blades."

I'm about to ask West to spill the goods on Mr. Slimeball when Willow's phone barks.

Literally barks.

"Oh, that's Daisy, my dog sitter." She grabs the phone from her purse and opens it at cheetah speed. "What? Wait, slow down, Dee," she says. "Sparky made a nest of my—"

Willow breaks off with a sigh, dropping her head to rest in her hand. "He does that sometimes. He grabs them all from the laundry. He has…a thing."

I meet West's eyes and mouth *fetish?*

Underwear fetish, he mouths back.

I bite my lip, stifling a giggle.

"Sure thing, Daisy, don't worry, I'll be right there." Willow pauses, then continues, "No, he usually doesn't eat things he shouldn't. When he starts gathering socks, it just means he's ready for me to put him to bed. He likes to be tucked in. So do the others. But I'll come home and keep an eye on him to make sure he hasn't been chewing on things he shouldn't."

West's mouth forms an O. *Socks, of course.*

Willow ends the call, her brow furrowing as she turns back to us. "I'm sorry, but I have to go. My chihuahuas. The sitter thinks Sparky might have eaten a sock while she wasn't looking. But I'll pay the check, and you guys can stay and finish," she says, gesturing to our half full plates.

I wouldn't mind finishing. I'm still famished.

"Are you sure?' West asks.

"Of course. Stay." She smiles as she slides out of the booth. "Thank you again—for the help and the chef talk. It was so fun. But Skippy, Salty, Stringbean, and Sparky aren't used to me being out after seven or eight. They get anxious."

"You have four dogs?" West asks.

Willow just shrugs and smiles. "Dogs like me."

"Smart dogs," I say.

She laughs—actually laughs without covering her mouth or hiding behind her hair—waves, pays the bill at the cashier, and heads out into the thickening twilight.

And then I'm alone with West again.

Just West. Gorgeous, kind, thoughtful fireman West.

But I'm not technically alone. Since we're in a restaurant. I'm safe from myself here. It's a diner, and a brightly lit one, at that. I'm not going to blow him under the table, for God's sake.

I'm *not* going to blow him under the table.

Right?

Swallowing hard I pluck a curly fry from my plate and point it West's way. "So, spill. What's the scoop on Hawley? Because I got a bad vibe from him from the start."

West's eyes narrow even as his lips curve up on one side. "I saw that. You've got good instincts."

I shrug. "Not always, but glad to know they were working today."

"Me too," he agrees. "Hawley's a garbage person. Comes from obscene old money but has never met a person he wouldn't screw over to get more. Cleary, he's a talented chef, but rumor has it he stole most of his best recipes—including the ones he's monetized—from his ex-girlfriends. For years, he only dated other pastry chefs." He sighs. "Until he started dating my sister a few years ago."

My jaw drops. "What? How did that happen, big brother?"

West sighs. "I know. I feel like shit that I didn't keep her away from him, but I didn't realize what a piece of shit he was until after he dumped her. Brutally. My instincts weren't so great where he was concerned." He picks up a fry, tossing it into his mouth and chewing before he adds, "Though, back then, I spent so much time with banker pricks who didn't care about anything but money that Hawley actually seemed okay in comparison. At least he had interests outside of acquiring more material possessions and vacation homes."

"Vacation *homes*," I echo with a shake of my head. "I

can't imagine having one of those, let alone multiples." I frown and grab another fry. "I mean, why would you really need more than one? Who can do that much vacationing?"

"Trust fund babies and men in line to inherit their father's wealth and title," he offers, with a hint of bitterness. "Though, honestly, even if I had more money than God, I can't imagine sitting around on a beach half the year and skiing the other. A person should do something worthwhile with his or her life. Otherwise, what's the point?"

I cock my head, charmed but in the mood to challenge him too. "So, you think running a tea shop is worthwhile?"

"I do," he says, looking surprised. "Don't you?"

I nod. "I do. People need warm, welcoming places to gather."

"And other people to take care of them and serve them delicious things that remind them of home," he says, sending another arrow directly into my heart.

I wrap my hands around my water glass. "Yes. Exactly. Or make them feel the way they *should* have felt at home—loved and safe and free to be themselves and enjoy it."

His gaze softens, and I feel myself pulled into the irresistible tractor beam of his West-vibe all over again. "Surely, someone as adorable as you must have been very loved."

I bob my shoulder. "My gram and brother are great, though he was pretty bossy when we were growing up. But that was just his way of trying to feel in control amidst the chaos. Our parents were…a lot. Most of it not good."

He frowns. "I'm sorry."

"It's okay," I say, brightening as I add, "My aunt and uncle and cousin are great too. And tons of people have things way worse."

"Still, I feel like a bit of a spoiled brat. My parents were both great. Dad's a bit analytical, but a solid chap who loves all four of his crazy kids to bits. And Mum was just…wonderful. Funny as hell, creative, and with the patience of a saint. Even when my brothers and I were wrestling in the house and breaking all her nice things."

I press my lips together but, in the end, can't help asking, "When did she pass?"

"A long time ago," he says with a smile that doesn't reach his eyes. "I was eighteen."

Under the table, I wrap my feet around his leg and give it a squeeze. "I'm sorry."

He takes my hand, threading his fingers through mine, making my chest feel even tighter. "Thanks. She was an amazing chef. It was her scone recipe that helped me snag that 8."

"Oh, West," I sigh, surprised to feel the back of my nose start to sting. "That's great. She would be so proud of you."

"I hope so. In any event, it was nice to have her with me today. That's why Abby and I quit our boring day jobs to open the shop. For Mum. It's been our secret plan since we were kids."

I press my free hand to my heart and whisper, "Stop it."

He arches a brow. "Stop what?"

"Stop being so...perfect."

He grins one of his wicked grins. "I'm far from perfect. I have many unlikeable qualities. I can be very bossy."

"Yes, I really hate that about you," I say dryly, pulling my hand from his and crossing my arms.

His low, sexy laugh makes it clear he knows I love his bossiness, especially in the bedroom. "And I'm impatient and judgmental, especially with people who don't share my values."

"Values are important." I find myself confessing, "As someone who's been cheated on by every serious boyfriend I've ever had, I get that. I need someone who shares my values."

West scowls, a dark look that actually makes me sit back in my chair. "What absolute pieces of shit. They all deserve to be castrated. Slowly and painfully."

I smile. "I think the painful part can probably be taken for granted with that. But thanks."

I take a breath, prepared to change the subject, when he says, "My last serious girlfriend saw me as more of a blank check than a boyfriend. Turned me off relationships, to be honest."

I need to make a mental note in Sharpie that West isn't looking for anything lasting. My squishy heart often wants more than a man can give. Must not forget he's happily single.

"That's understandable, wanting to steer clear of

anything complicated." I don't want him to think I'm a clinger. I want him to know I understand the score. I respect his stance.

He motions toward himself. "Plus, not to brag, but I have several other excellent qualities on offer aside from my bottom line."

I nod. "You really do."

He frowns. "You don't sound convinced."

"No, you absolutely do. You're great." I pick at my napkin as I add, "I'm glad we're friends."

Friends.

We. Are. Just. Friends.

And that might be all we'll ever be. He's not interested in a relationship. He made that clear the night we met, and he just underlined it in red ink. And I can't blame him for feeling that way, not when I said the same thing myself.

But I'm starting to realize that if I spend much more time with West, I'm going to fall in love with him. Deeply, wildly, *madly* in love. He checks so many of my boxes. Add in the fact that he's so kind and willing to be vulnerable and calls me "adorable" in a way that makes me believe he really means it, and I'm on a collision course with heartache.

Not to mention having my focus shot to hell right when I need it most. If I don't blow past him at the challenge in four days, I won't have a chance of winning Mrs. Sweets.

But when he says, "So, friend, would you want to come to mine for a nightcap? I promise I'll send you home in plenty of time to get your beauty sleep," I find myself nodding and sliding out of the booth.

Just one drink.

How much trouble can I get into during one teensy tiny little drink?

12

GIGI

The answer is two fingers.

As in two fingers worth of whiskey in this Sazerac.

This heavenly, disgustingly good cocktail, both sweet and bitter, that's taking the express lane to my head.

I tap the glass. "This is officially unfair." I kick a petulant foot back and forth as I sink into the plush gray couch in West's—I can't believe I'm saying this —*library*.

The man has a freaking library.

With floor-to-ceiling shelves. And old books. And new books. And a ladder.

I just can't.

I might come just from staring at the books.

But I'd rather stare at the man who can mix drinks as well as he bakes.

"What's not fair, love?" West knocks back some of his drink then sets it down on the table next to my purse, cupping my knee with his warm hand, sending a rush of tingles through me.

Tingles that settle between my breasts, making my nipples hard.

So does the idea of banging on that ladder.

"First, the library. Second"—I gesture his way —"your face. Third, the drink, which is divine. All of it, unfair."

I take another tiny sip, and he laughs, making me pout. "Are you laughing at the way I drink?"

"Are you laughing at my face? My *unfair* face?" He squeezes my knee harder.

Another flurry of shivers runs down my spine.

My gaze drifts down to his hand on my leg, then my thoughts traipse back to the diner, to the warning I gave myself.

I'm not going to blow him under the table.

And you know what? I didn't.

I'm going to blow him in his library instead.

When I made that promise I had no idea the trifecta of whiskey-library-face seduction I'd be up against! No one in their right mind could fault me for breaking under this kind of pressure.

I finish my drink in a gulp, savoring the last drops of the lemon, the syrup, the bitters, letting them swirl on my tongue as I imagine other last drops.

A glint of curiosity crosses West's dark eyes. "What's on your mind?"

"Why would you think I have something on my mind?"

"Your eyes are ripping my clothes off." He practically rumbles the words—a dirty, English rumble.

I set down the glass, feeling bold, feeling beautiful. Maybe it's the drink. Maybe it's West.

Maybe it's me.

Whatever the reason, I *want*.

I want him. But I can't lose myself in this man, so I choose my weapons wisely.

My mouth. That's it. And I chart the course.

I slide a hand up his pants on a fast track for the thickening bulge that has *all* my attention. "I have a confession," I whisper as I cover the hard ridge of his cock with my palm.

My breath catches; his hitches.

"By all means, *confess*. And I mean that in the bossiest of ways." His husky voice makes a pulse beat faster between my legs.

I squeeze his cock harder, then I slide down to the floor. "I didn't say yes to the drink because I was thirsty." I work open the buttons, slide down the zipper.

"Let me guess, beautiful." He slides a big hand through my hair, curling it around my head possessively, oh so possessively. "You came here because you were hungry? Hungry for my cock?"

A full-body shudder seizes me from head to toe, electrifies my cells. "Dirty talker."

"Filthy," he promises.

Damn. *Yes*, I could fall for this man.

But like this, on my knees, I'm in control of the moment.

And oddly enough, of my heart.

This is all I'll allow.

The chance to please him.

I won't be giving in to my soft heart if I take his hard cock to the back of my throat. I'll just be giving in to my basest desires.

Those have a hold of me right now, and I don't want them to let go.

He pushes his pants down his hips, to his thighs, gripping the base.

I lick my lips, then make a split-second decision. Reaching for my purse, I dip a hand into it and fish out a kinky baker girl's best friend—a long, pink polka dot cloth headband that I use to hold my hair back by day.

And that West can use to pin my wrists with by night.

I dangle it in front of me. "I said I liked scarves."

"But hair ties will do just fine," he finishes, then makes a circling gesture with his finger.

I rise, turn around, and let the man bind my wrists behind my back.

Then I return to the floor, kneel before him, and give him my only order. "Like you said, I'm hungry. Please feed me your cock."

13

WEST

Gladly.

And with so much pleasure.

Gripping the base, I offer my cock to the woman in the red dress.

The one on her knees.

Between my legs.

Asking for my dick to slide between her lips.

This is clearly a dream. The most authentic, lifelike, intensely real dream I've ever had. I watch Gigi part those red lips and practically beg for me to fill her mouth.

I push in the crown, and she wraps her lips around my dick like she's just tasted the most succulent dessert. Groaning, I curl a hand through her hair. "That's right, beautiful," I murmur as she draws me in deeper, swirling her tongue over the head, sending bolts of pleasure straight to my balls.

She hums around my shaft as she takes me in

farther, bringing me deeper into the warm paradise of her mouth.

A shudder wracks me as Gigi opens wider, flicking her tongue as I slide home, and then, she takes me to the back of her throat on a sexy, needy pant.

Her eyes float closed, and she looks enraptured.

I am on fire.

Flames lick my skin.

Sparks cover my body.

I don't know what I ever did to deserve this kind of treatment, but I need to find out and do it again and again. "Yes, nice and deep, beautiful. That's so fucking perfect," I rasp, clutching her head, sliding my other hand through her hair, too.

I guide her through the blow job, the way she asked me to do when she told me to tie her up. It's a filthy sight. This goddess trussed up, mouth wide open, lavishing fantastic attention on my cock.

As I control her.

As I grip her head.

As I set the pace.

Like she wants me to.

My sweet, submissive—but always on her terms—dirty, little lover.

My thighs burn with pleasure as Gigi licks and sucks, doing all the work. As she swirls her tongue, I punch up my hips, wanting to fill her mouth, to thrust deep.

But a gentleman should make sure such advances are welcome.

"Can I fuck your mouth, love?"

Her answer comes in sparks in her blue eyes, and a speedy nod.

With her permission, I nudge my cock deeper, grip her tighter, and thrust.

I fuck her gorgeous lips, watching her cheeks hollow out, as Gigi takes and takes and I give and give, until my balls tighten, and pleasure charges down my spine, barreling through my body.

"Yes. Fucking yes. Coming. Coming now." I squeeze my eyes shut as my orgasm pummels me with excruciatingly blissful force.

It annihilates my senses, frying brain cells.

When I open my eyes and stop shaking, I smile woozily at the scene in front of me.

Gigi, with wild intent in her gaze.

Her lips parted.

Her thighs squeezing.

"I need to make you come, love," I tell her. Since she likes my bossy side, I give her an order. "Stay on your knees."

"Yes, sir," she says in a salacious tone.

I tug up my briefs and trousers and move behind her, freeing her wrists.

"Hands and arms in front of you, on the couch," I say, and she stretches forward, reaching her arms to the edge of the cushion.

Like a good girl, she lifts her lovely arse up, granting me full access.

I move behind her, one knee on the floor, one knee bent, and I yank her knickers to the side to sweep my fingers across her hot, wet pussy.

Fuck, she feels fantastic.

Slippery and warm and so ready.

"Oh, God," she groans, offering me more, lifting her arse even higher.

Like that, I fuck her with my fingers, thrusting one, then two into her sweetness, playing with her, filling her.

With a moan, her head falls forward, her hips arching and swaying.

But I know she wants more than fingers.

She wants hands on flesh.

I raise my left palm and bring it down hard on her cheek.

She gasps.

I rub another finger against her clit.

Then lift my hand once more, swatting her again.

Another feral moan.

I crook my fingers, hitting that spot that makes her shake. That makes her legs tremble. That makes her cry out.

One more sharp smack, one deep thrust, then she's falling apart, coming undone, calling my name.

She pants and writhes then sinks down to the floor.

I press a gentle kiss to her bottom. Then one more, savoring the soft skin. I rub gently where I hit her, soothing any ache.

She turns her face to the side, looking lust-drunk and so damn happy. "That was yummy."

"Maybe now you'll spend the night in my unfair library. Or, better yet, in my unfair bed, and I can feed you something unfairly fantastic for breakfast?"

I wait, hoping so damn hard. Wanting her yes more than I could have imagined.

Her face softens even more, the expression so lovely and inviting.

Perhaps I've convinced her.

I don't breathe for a few seconds.

But she's a lion underneath. She shakes her head, shudders out a *no*. "I want to, but I have to go. The longer I stay, the more I'll never want to leave."

She gathers her things, and she...goes.

Dammit.

14

From the texts of Gigi James and West Byron

West: Have you made it home safely, love? I expect a text when you're all tucked in for the night.

Gigi: Bossy, bossy. *winking emoji* All tucked in, sir.

West: Fuck.

Gigi: No, we don't do that. We're just friends, remember?

West: Friends who fuck? Please say we're friends who fuck. As lovely as everything else tonight was—and it was absolutely fucking lovely—I'm still lying here hard as a day-old scone, dying to be inside you.

Gigi: Considering scones are pretty hard to start with, that sounds serious.

West: My scones are never hard. They're firm and flaky, yet delightfully dense. Come over, and I'll feed you one. You'll see.

Gigi: No offense, but I'm not into scones, either. You'd have to tie me up and hold my nose.

West: That can be arranged…

Gigi: Nope. That's enough of that. Tonight was fun, but we have to focus. The next event is in four days. Four days, West! And I want to beat you fair and square, not because I kept you up for seventy-two hours straight riding you like a cowgirl at her last rodeo.

West: You. Cowgirl hat. Nothing else. I'm ordering one first thing in the morning.

Gigi: LOL. Go to sleep! That's what I'm going to do. My focus is where it's supposed to be—on the contest, not your cock.

West: Or your pussy.

Gigi: Or your hands on my ass.

West: Or the way your throat works when you swallow.

Gigi: God. I loved swallowing you. That whole thing was…so hot.

West: What was that? Sorry. I'd love to discuss that with you further, but a wise woman told me I should focus on handing her her ass in the kitchen, not smacking her ass in the library.

Gigi: Speaking of libraries.

West: Oh, did that get a rise out of you?

Gigi: Well, I do like books. And you have so many. And so many big books.

West: I'm glad you were admiring my big books, along with my tall shelves.

Gigi: Seriously, though! A girl could get lost in that library. I could spend hours curled up on that couch, escaping into a story. I'd devour one, then the next one, then another.

West: So, you're like Belle.

Gigi: Be still my beating heart. You know your princesses.

West: I would write LOL if I were an LOL-er. But yes, I do know the basic pop culture references, thank you.

Also, I have a younger sister who loves them. But it raises the question—am I the beast?

Gigi: The beast is my favorite hero. Want to know why?

West: The library.

Gigi: Actually, that's only half of it. Once you get past the whole keeping her prisoner thing, he's so...real. He has so much to overcome. His anger, his pride, his uncertainty.

West: True. He's not even sure how to eat appropriately, if memory serves? Doesn't she teach him table manners?

Gigi: Yes. AND THEN HE REPENTS near the end! Gah. When he realizes he was wrong to keep her and lets her go to see her father, I DIE every time. I SWOON. For a beast. He's so flawed and real. Therefore, I don't just love him for his library. I love him for his heart.

West: You're quite passionate about this beast.

Gigi: I'm passionate about most things. In case you haven't noticed.

West: Oh, I've noticed. And I approve. Though, I'm glad you didn't pick Snow White's Prince as your favorite. If you had, we might not be able to see each other again.

Gigi: What? Why would I? He's the most boring prince ever.

West: Right? Could he be any duller? He doesn't even have a name.

Gigi: I call him Prince Dullsworth the Lame Who Has a Weirdly Red Mouth. Also—did you just say you'd stop seeing me if I liked the wrong prince?

West: Yes. I did. I have standards, Gigi.

Gigi: Standards are hot, Prince Panty-Melter of Brooklyn Who Has a Ladder in His Library.
P.S. That sounded dirty, didn't it?

West: Yes, and I expect nothing less from you, Princess Kinky Who Wants to Fuck on My Ladder.

Gigi: Now I know what I'll dream of tonight…

West: And on that naughty note, I must go. Get my beauty sleep. Plot world dessert domination. That sort of thing.

Gigi: So, it's sleep that makes you so pretty? Good to know. Sleep well.

West: Goodnight, beautiful. See you soon.

Gigi: Soon.

15

GIGI

I can do this. No problem.

No conflict of interest.

No violation of my Rules of Engagement.

There's no reason I can't pop by a chocolate shop and buy a few gifts for my friends.

Warning my staff the next day that I might be late returning from lunch, I swing out of Sweetie Pies into the warm summer sun and stroll the few blocks over to Cocoa is Love. It's a perfect day for purchasing a few completely friendly gifts for people who are *all* just friends and family.

Pushing open the door, I step into the air-conditioned shop and inhale the mouth-watering scent of really good chocolate.

I say hi to the woman in linen behind the counter then begin my hunt. Perusing the shelves, I consider each bar with care. That's what shopping for others is—a chance to show them that you've taken the time to learn what makes them tick.

For Harrison, it's a chili pepper chocolate bar. He says chocolate gives him super-powered editing energy, and the peppers will give him an extra edge with his evil red pen, *mwahahaha*. I find a bar infused with grapefruit zest and, despite my personal reservations, add it to my basket for Gram, that crazy grapefruit lover. Next, I grab a bar of chocolate with dried cherries for Ruby—cherries are her favorite, but not maraschino cherries because, *eww*—and a few mini variety bars for my hardworking staff.

With that done, I move on to my next gift selection.

Just one of the *many* I'm here to purchase today. Not the entire reason I made a special trip to the chocolate shop *at all*.

Eyes darting around, I check the shop for witnesses like I'm about to dip my hand into the cookie jar.

But I'm being ridiculous, of course. Buying a gift for West is nothing to be secretive about. I'm simply repaying his thoughtfulness.

Tit for tat.

Mmm, I do like his hands on my tits, and he would be so hot with a tattoo. Even if it was something silly like a teapot on his bicep. He's hot enough to pull off a teapot tattoo.

"Just friends" thoughts, woman! You. Are. Just. Friends.

Right. Friends.

Forcing my thoughts to less seductive things than West's biceps—like tea and how gross it is and how only a monster would add it to chocolate, I scan the "smoky sweet" shelf.

I spot a bar named *No Grey Area Here* and can't help

but smile. Gross flavor combo, but an adorable name. Very Harrison-esque. And hey, if I'm thinking about my brother as I slip this bar from the shelf, that proves that West and I are simply pals who flirt and misbehave with our mouths once in a while.

As the bell dings above the door, I turn the bar over and read the description. He said he loved an Earl Grey infused chocolate, and this description certainly seems to fit the bill.

"This Earl Grey semi-sweet will steep your mouth in bliss and convince you sweet treats are made of teas," I read aloud.

A throat clears.

I jump and spin to see Ruby standing by the door.

She's with her mother—Aunt Barb, my mom's sister.

Shoulders tightening like I've been caught stealing, I instinctively swing my basket behind my back.

"Don't worry," Ruby calls. "We didn't see you hide a chocolate stash behind your back."

"Chocolate is nothing to be ashamed of, sweetheart," Barb says in her cheery voice. "We all love chocolate."

"Unless you've got more than four bars in there, then you might have a problem," Ruby teases.

"Stop trying to sweet-shame me, you cherry addict," I tease right back. "And move away from the counter. I might have a little treat in here for you that I don't want you to see yet."

Laughing, Ruby blows me a kiss. "You're the best. Come see us before you leave."

"Will do," I promise. As Ruby and Barb grab a table in the café section—frozen chocolate drinks are one of their summer traditions—I settle up at the counter and collect my pink bag of treasures.

When I turn to see Ruby and Barb laughing as they open their menus, my heart squeezes a little bit. I always wished I had that kind of relationship with my mom. That we were the kind of mother-daughter pair who hung out at cafés laughing, eating, and telling stories.

Just hanging out together on a Tuesday.

I wish I knew what that was like. But at least I have Aunt Barb and Gram.

When I join them, Barb extends an arm my way. "Hey there, sugar, how are you? You've been working so hard, I feel like I barely see you anymore. You should come over for dinner soon and let me feed you."

"Yes," Ruby agrees. "Feed both of us, please. Coconut curry chicken like when we were little."

I moan in remembered bliss. "Oh yes. Please."

Barb laughs. "Done. And then we'll take dessert out to the garden and watch the stars come out."

"Speaking of dessert," Ruby says, patting the table. "Show me the goods, girl."

I tut at her. "You must be terrible at Christmas." I pause, putting a mock-thoughtful finger to my lips. "Oh, wait. You are. You peek at all your gifts like a devious little spy who can't be trusted in my apartment alone."

"It's only because *you're* so good at giving presents." She makes grabby hands. "So, let me see, let me see."

"Terrible," I say. "And when I know you were raised so well."

"I did try," Barb says with a laugh.

"How will I know what to order *now* if I don't know

what Gigi's gifting me later?" Ruby's lips push into a pout, and I relent.

I love giving gifts, especially to grateful and excited recipients like my cousin. I hand over the bag, and Ruby coos and thanks me before peering inside. "Yay cherries for me! And Harrison is going to love that chili number, but who's *that* for?"

She points at the *No Grey Area Here* bar.

"No one special," I say breezily. "Just another friend. No one you know."

Ruby straightens and stares at me, a wicked smile spreading slowly across her face. "You bought that for a man, didn't you?"

I huff. "Yes, a man who is a friend."

"No, this is a man you *like*. You wanted to buy him a treat but didn't want to feel weird about it, so you hid his present in with all the friend gifts to trick yourself into deciding it was okay to buy him an 'I like you' present," she says, seeing inside my guilty little soul.

"That's some serious psychology," Barb says, a Sherlock Holmes tone to her voice.

A flush creeps up my neck.

I've been caught.

And even though deep down I knew all along this was a West-focused mission, having Ruby lay it all out there is still...uncomfortable.

Like being caught with nothing but socks on—the rest of you feels even more naked somehow.

Dangerously naked.

It's *dangerous* to like a man enough that you go hunting gross chocolate just for him.

Ugh. What am I doing? Especially when West made it clear he isn't up for anything but a fling?

"It's for the man who's opening Tea and Empathy, isn't it?" Ruby asks with a knowing quirk of her brow.

I wrinkle my nose. "Yes."

"Oh, *him*. He's really something," Barb says, her eyes going wide. "I saw him carrying some paint into his shop the other morning on my walk. Just a stunning man. I bet he already gets marriage proposals slipped under the shop door."

A spark of jealousy ignites in my chest. "He better not," I mutter.

Ruby cracks up.

So does Barb.

Then Ruby gives me a long, exaggerated nod. "Never mind. I was mistaken, he's *clearly* just a man who's your friend."

Barb pats my hand. "I'm sure he'll be fooled, too." With a wink, she slips out of her chair. "Be right back, girls. I need to go talk to Linda about a bulk order for the pies I'm cooking for the Boys and Girls Club fundraiser next week."

As soon as she's out of ear shot, Ruby grabs my arm. "Liar, liar, pants on fire. I didn't want to spill the beans in front of Mom, but you slept with the competition again. Didn't you!"

Heaving a tortured sigh, I cave, pouring out my insides like a snowman melting on a summer day. "Sort of, but Ruby, I couldn't help myself. He can solve a Rubik's Cube in under a minute. He looks and sounds just like Henry Cavill. He's smart and clever and filthy in bed, and he can cook like nobody's business and he's sweet to shy people, and to me, and I'm just —"

"A cruel, terrible person," she finishes.

I blink. "What? Why am I cruel and terrible?"

"Because you didn't call me to tell me about all this! I thought Weston was still *persona non grata*. I thought we were still hating him until the end of time or not talking about him because it was upsetting to you or whatever." She nudges my arm. "You should have told me you'd had a change of heart and maybe even…" She hesitates before continuing in a hopeful whisper, "found the man of your dreams?"

I shake my head. "He's not the man of my dreams."

"Stop. You've already withheld yummy gossip from your best friend and favorite cousin," she says, "don't add fibbing to your list of sins."

I press my lips together, at war with myself, and my chest is suddenly so tight it's hard to breathe.

"Hey, babe," Ruby adds in a softer, more serious voice as she lays gentle fingers on my arm. "I'm just kidding. You don't have to talk about this if you don't want to. Your romantic business is *your* romantic business, not anyone else's."

"It's not that," I say, biting the side of my mouth. "It's…everything. Everything is dumb."

"Everything?" She arches a brow. "Would it help to maybe break that down a little?"

I take a fortifying breath. "Okay, one, he's in the competition, and I can feel myself getting distracted by him. And I can't afford distraction, not when I barely squeaked into the top three in the first challenge. I have to stay strong, or I won't have a chance in hell of winning. Two, even if he wasn't in the competition, or after the competition is over, don't you think getting involved with the guy across the street is a tiny bit dumb?"

Ruby hums thoughtfully. "Because you'll have to see him every day if it doesn't work out?"

My heart sinks even lower. "Yes. And really, what are the chances it will work out? Even if I can convince him to give serious dating a try, things never work out with me and boyfriends. Boyfriends always break my heart. *Always.* The only saving grace is that we live in a huge city and I usually don't have to see them again."

At least not every day. I've run into Theodore on the street and that was misery, and I bumped into Shelby on the subway. The *same* car. Thank God, I never see Nelson the Odious since he doesn't deign to come to Brooklyn.

Which brings me to my point.

"If I truly pursue something with West"—I shudder —"can you imagine how awful it would be to see him right across the street, going about his life without me? Happy that I'm no longer in his bed? Maybe even bringing his new girlfriend to his shop for brunch because *of course* she's perfect for him and beautiful and sweet and loves gross, disgusting tea as much as he does." I press my hand to the ache in my chest. "God. It hurts just thinking about it."

Truly, it does.

I can feel it already, how much my heart will break when West disappoints me.

When, not *if*. I'd love to believe he's different than the men who've betrayed me in the past, but I've been burned so many times.

And how much more would those burns have hurt if I'd been forced to see those men's faces every day?

Ruby takes my hand. "It's a valid concern. That would be really hard, but…"

"But?" I prod after a moment.

"But maybe worth the risk?"

I gulp. "I think friends is better. Friends. At least for now."

Ruby's lips part, but before she can speak, Aunt Barb returns, and the discussion veers to pies and charity work, and before I know it, I'm on my way back to the store to clear a space in my baking schedule for my own donation to the Boys and Girls Club auction.

I concentrate on paying it forward to my community and ignore the tangle of confusion knotting my stomach as I slip West's present into his mail slot with a note that reads, "Something sweet to go with your dirty."

* * *

Later that night, West sends me a text.

West: This chocolate is almost as delicious as you are.

And I swoon.

But it's a friendly swoon, I swear.

16

WEST

I devour the chocolate she sent me, savoring every bite the way I intend to savor her pussy the next time I'm between her thighs, and wait for a text back.

I'm still waiting the next morning as I head into the shop to put the finishing touches on plans for opening day.

But still she doesn't respond.

Not so much as an emoji.

I'm not happy. But I don't suspect she's playing games. Even when she was angry with me, she was frank about it. She didn't give me the silent treatment or play the "guess why I'm mad" game. She laid it out for me, right on the street, no less.

Gigi James doesn't mince words. She wears her heart on her sleeve and she uses that mouth.

Dear God, that mouth.

She also spoke plainly after the blow job in my library too, making it clear that we can't be more than friends who...*don't* fuck, but do things that are very fuck-adjacent.

A tad confusing, maybe. But honest.

There's something so refreshing about that level of honesty.

There's something wildly appealing too, about her reasons—her laser focus on her family's business is commendable. Yet another reason to like her.

Dammit. I wish there weren't so many. It would be a hell of a lot easier to keep my focus where it belongs—on a successful opening Friday and a solid performance at the next challenge .

It's like I always say, timing is everything. And Gigi's made it clear that now is not the time for anything to happen with the man across the street.

* * *

I'm still thinking about timing a few hours later as I'm walking toward Sweetie Pies on my way home and Gigi suddenly charges out onto the sidewalk and shouts, "Ms. Milton, you forgot your change!"

An older woman across the street waiting by the bus stop waves a hand. "Oh, you keep it, dear. You do such a good job."

Gigi smiles, but shakes her head. "You're so sweet, but this is a... large tip. I think you may have left the wrong bill by mistake."

The woman's smile crinkles her face in a clearly familiar pattern of wrinkles that's rather beautiful. "Oh, take the hundred dollars, sweetheart, and go buy yourself something nice. You deserve it. Your pie and sweet smile are the best part of my week."

"Oh my goodness, well, thank you." Gigi presses a hand to her chest. "Thank you so much."

She's still standing there with her hand over her heart as Ms. Milton's bus swallows her up and trundles her away.

I wait until the sound of the engine fades before I say, "Boo."

Gigi jumps and turns my way, revealing the tears shining in her eyes. Before I realize I'm moving, I'm beside her, resting a gentle hand on her back. "Hey, there, love. What's wrong? I saw what happened with your patron. That wasn't a nice thing to hear?"

"No, it was, I just..." She shakes her head, her chin trembling for a moment before she says, "I love that I'm the best part of her week, but I hate it too. People should have better things than pie in their life. You know? They should have people who love them and bring them joy."

Brow furrowing, I nod. "Yes, they should. But we don't always get what we deserve. For good or for ill."

She sniffs. "No, but she should still have someone. Ms. Milton is wonderful." She swallows hard and lifts her chin, meeting my gaze with a look I've never seen in her eyes before.

She's so...serious.

And even more real and honest. And in that moment, I decide to do whatever it takes for her to trust me with this look again.

I adore funny, sexy, kinky Gigi, but this woman with her heart in her eyes is irresistible.

"Tell me," I say softly. "Whatever it is. You can trust me, friend."

"But that's the thing. I don't know if I can just be your friend," she says. "And that's...scary."

"Why?" I ask. "I don't bite. Not unless you ask nicely and tell me how hard you like it."

She doesn't so much as blink, let alone smile.

I cup her face, sobering. "I know. You're right. It *is* scary. People do horrible things to each other when they're dating, things they'd never do to a friend."

"Right," she says. "When it should be the other way around. You should be more kind and careful with the people who let you that close, not more awful."

"Agreed. But I won't do those horrible things, Gigi. I don't play those kinds of games. I don't play games, period, unless they come in a box. So, would you want to come back to my place tonight and play Scrabble with me? And let me make you dinner and show you that we can be friends who care about each other and have extraordinary sex and the sky won't come falling down?"

She holds my gaze and everything in the background goes soft until her lovely face is the only thing in focus.

Finally, she whispers, "Monopoly not Scrabble." She steps closer, then turns her head toward my ear. "And the winner picks the location for the main attraction."

When she pulls away, her eyes look wicked, but sweet, too.

How is that possible?

How can Gigi be so vulnerable with her heart and so naughty with her mouth? But that's the onion of this woman. And I happen to like onions.

I grab her hand, tug her close, and brush my lips to hers. "See you at eight."

"I'll be there." When we break the kiss, the vixen of seconds ago has vanished. In her place is the woman who said people should be kind. That's the woman who flashes me a nervous smile but then squares her shoulders and lifts her chin. "And if you invite me to spend the night, I'll say yes."

Answering her unspoken question isn't hard at all. "You damn well better."

17

From the texts of Gigi James and West Byron

Gigi: Guess where I am?

West: Since it's 7:55, you'd better be five minutes away. Unless you're naked in the bath and want to send photos. I will accept tardiness in that case.

Gigi: You like tub photos? Noted.

West: I like YOU photos. *Note that.*

Gigi: Then, just imagine I'm sending you a picture of me walking out of the wine shop two blocks from your place with a fantastic chardonnay for the chicken you're making. Because this wine pairs very well with chicken, though honestly, I bought it because I thought it would pair well with your lips.

West: I like your thinking, woman.

Gigi: I also brought a peach pie. Because…peach pie.

West: Peach pie needs no explanation.

Gigi: And I don't have to be at work until ten tomorrow.

West: Brilliant.

Gigi: Also, West?

West: Yes?

Gigi: I never responded to your text from last night. About the chocolate.

West: You're not required to respond.

Gigi: I know. But if I were you, I would have wanted a response. I was honestly just…a little scared.

West: Of what?

Gigi: That if I texted back, I'd confess how much I loved buying you a little gift. Picking it out and hoping you'd like it. Hoping that you'd think of me.

West: I loved it, Gigi, and I absolutely thought of you. I think of you often.

Gigi: Good. Because here I am, ringing your bell.

West: Oh, you are definitely ringing my bell.

Dreams coming true.

I swear I can see them taunting me from just over the hill. Peeking around the corner. Poking their head out like a groundhog in February searching for spring.

I have a wild, loop-de-loop feeling in my chest and suspect that Dreams Coming True might taste even better than the peach pie I brought for dessert.

But first, I indulge in West's yummy buttermilk-marinated roast chicken and sautéed broccolini and, *gasp*, bread.

Homemade bread.

It's warm and yeasty and pillowy. I rip off a hunk and pop it into my mouth. I lick my lips, delighted that my *boyf*—nope, he's my *date*, that's all—can cook this well.

"If your scones taste anything like this bread, I might have to revisit my feelings about them," I say after I finish chewing. We're at the counter in his kitchen, perched on wooden bar stools, surrounded by his fantastic cooking.

Lifting his wine glass, he arches a wry brow. "If you mean that my scones are heavenly, mouth-watering and delicious, you'd be right." He takes a drink of the wine, then sets it down. "I'm looking forward to you rescinding all those horrid things you said."

I give him a saucy look. "You'll have to prove they're as good as this bread."

He drops a kiss to my cheek. "That means you'll have to come over again."

My breath catches. He asked me for another date.

Though, really, tonight is basically a hookup.

A hookup with yummy food and board games, but still... I shouldn't jump to conclusions.

Except, those familiar play-it-cool tricks aren't working. I can't fool myself any longer, and I don't really want to. Tonight feels like so much more than casual sex.

At least, it does to me.

So...this is a real date.

And he just asked me on another one.

I give him the only answer I can. "Then I say yes."

He cups my cheek and brushes his lips to mine, sending the world spiraling away in a dazzling wine-soaked kiss.

But soon, he breaks it. "Time for Monopoly. Fair warning, if I don't win in thirty minutes, I'm likely to forfeit because I don't know how long I can wait to have you, love."

I tap his nose lightly with my finger. "Good things come to those who wait."

But I don't want him to wait. I really don't.

* * *

"I'm close. So close." I shimmy my shoulders in a near-victory dance as he places the race car on Boardwalk. "I am a hotel magnate! Pay up, mister. Pay up!"

I rub my thumb and forefinger together.

He grumbles but turns over several bills. "You are terrible," he says from our spot on the couch in his library, the game spread out on the coffee table.

"I know, but I'm a very benevolent hotel owner, and if you play your cards right, you might get the room service special." I give him an over-the-top wink as I waggle the fake bills.

I punctuate my showboating by leaning closer to give my sexy Brit a hot smooch.

I can't even blame the wine. I only had one glass. But I'm feeling so bubbly. So effervescent.

I want to kiss him and touch him and talk to him. I want to play games, tell him my stories, hear all of his. And I want to go to bed with him very soon.

"Also, don't feel bad," I add. "You're a fantastic competitor. Losing doesn't change that."

"I haven't lost yet, woman," he growls, all tough and broody.

"But you will. Oh, mark my words, West Byron, you will."

"You and my sister," he mutters.

"Aww. Did Abby school you in Monopoly, too?"

"She absolutely did. She was ferocious, made me play for hours." He says it with a huff, but it's clear he loved every second of those games.

"And you couldn't resist her. You always said yes to your little sister, I bet."

He simply shrugs and smiles. "What can I say? She had me wrapped around her little finger. I'd give her the world if I could."

My heart thunders.

I remember what my gram used to say to Harrison when we were growing up. "You can tell the measure of a man by how he treats his sister. That's how he'll treat his partner."

The way West is with Abby—the things he does for her, how he prioritizes her—tugs on my heart so much. Makes me want to take my heart out of the gilded cage that I've kept it in lately and offer it to him, let him care for it.

I cover my heart with my hand, my throat tightening. "I love that you love your sister so much. That you look out for her, and that you always did," I blurt out.

West laughs, but then it fades as he tilts his head, locking his eyes with mine. "You do?"

"Yeah, I do. I think it's wonderful. I've known men who don't talk to their families or their sisters at all. Or who are just flat-out mean or disrespectful. But the way you are is really wonderful."

"It's the only way to be." He brushes a lock of hair

from my cheek, even though I don't think my hair is out of place. "And I love that you're such a people person, Gigi," he says, his rich, warm voice like honey.

"Good. Because I can't help it." I laugh, casting my eyes down.

Tucking a finger under my chin, he raises my face. "It's wildly endearing. The way you think about others. How you care about strangers and family and friends. Even people you haven't met, like my sister. It's so…" It almost seems like he's going to say *sexy*, but he stops himself, and takes his time with the next word. "Beautiful."

My heart thumps against my chest, emotions welling. "West, what you said earlier on the street? About games?"

"Yes?"

I steady myself to strip bare in a way that scares me so much more than *actual* stripping. "I don't want to play games, either. I'm glad you don't like that stuff."

"I don't. At all. I like honesty, even when it's hard."

"So do I." My pulse spikes. I am caught in his orbit, and I don't want to be anywhere else. "Also, I forfeit."

"You don't want to finish the game?" he asks, bending closer to me on the couch, dusting his lips across my cheek.

I swear this wasn't supposed to happen. I met him and planned to sleep with him, and that was all. But now, just a few days later, I'm swimming in a sea of feelings.

There's only one solution.

Keep going.

I tug him up from the couch, my hand in his. "The ladder."

His dark eyes shine with dirty deeds. "Perfect location."

19

WEST

I begin my confession as I undress her. First, I slide the straps of her red and white polka-dot dress over her shoulders, down her arms. "Since the first night I met you, I've wanted to have you here."

"On your ladder?" She reaches for the hem of my navy-blue polo shirt.

I bury my face in her neck, inhaling her flower-and-sweet-spice scent, letting it flood my senses.

"Yes. And my tub, and my couch, and my pool table."

"Sounds like a game of Clue—Gigi, in the library, with your cock," she says with a light laugh, and I love that she can be passionate and funny in the same moment.

I return to removing every item of clothing from her gorgeous body.

Down goes the bodice, off goes the skirt, then the shoes, until she wears only her lacy underthings—a pretty pink bra that boosts those lush breasts, and matching knickers that I bet are as soaked as I am hard.

But arousal is not all I see on Gigi.

That's just the surface. A surface I adore. But I'm adoring too, what's inside her. What's under her skin, in her heart, percolating in that quick mind.

She's clever and kind, and it's a flavor combination I never knew I wanted, but now I need to taste over and over.

"Gigi James, you're irresistible," I tell her, as I reach for her wrists, lift them over her head, and tell her to hold onto the rung.

She curls her palms around it. "Like this?"

"Yes, that's perfect. I've pictured this so many times."

I kiss the hollow of her throat, eliciting a gasp, then her shoulder, drawing an arch of her gorgeous back. Slowly, luxuriously, I make my way down her arm to the crook of her elbow, brushing soft, tender kisses along her skin. "Your skin is so soft," I whisper. "I could kiss you everywhere."

"I won't stop you, West."

I crave the way she says my name at times like this, all heated and needy, like she desperately needs me to please her body.

But also like she needs *me*.

Just me.

As I travel back up her arm, down her chest, burying my face between the lush valley of these gorgeous globes, I feel so much need for her.

But it's more than sexual.

I need this woman with me. In my house. My life.

I didn't set out to find a woman who captivated me.

Or to meet someone I'd become consumed with. But in a shockingly short while, that's exactly what I've found.

A woman who challenges all my assumptions about myself.

My belief in my independence.

My certainty that I don't want a relationship.

My steadfast faith that timing is everything.

The timing for us feels all wrong.

But everything is so right with her.

I don't know what happens tomorrow or the next day or the day after, but I know this much—I want her with me for far longer than a week or two. And I want her as more than a friend.

And that means tonight is not the night to fuck her on a ladder.

It's the night to make love to her in my bed.

I raise my face and look into her gorgeous blue eyes, shimmering with desire and so much more.

"Wrap your arms around my neck, darling."

She does. "Why?"

"So you can come to my bed, where I can worship your body properly. So I can spread you out and lavish attention on you. And mostly, so I can show you how much I want you in my life."

She shivers and parts her lips.

20

GIGI

I don't know how to speak without my voice breaking, without starting to cry.

But not tears of sadness.

Tears of wonder.

Wonder at how this happened so quickly, so spectacularly.

But I don't want to mar this moment with sniffles, so I swallow past the knot in my throat, and speak with a tremble in my voice but with all the certainty in the world. "I want you in my life too." I loop my arms tighter around his neck. "As more than a friend."

He slides his hands under my ass, scoops me up, angling me so I can wrap my legs around his waist. "You're already more than a friend," he says, those dark eyes intent on mine as he carries me to his bedroom, sets me on his king size bed and strips off my bra and panties.

His hands are strong, but gentle too, as if I'm something he cherishes. As he slides his hands down my body, trailing them over my skin, I feel adored.

He looks at me like he wants so much more than one night. Like he wants time and memories and plans for the future.

And I want all the same things.

Starting right now.

I sit up and help him along, tugging at his shirt. I yank it over his head as he unzips his pants. "Eager much?" he teases.

"So eager. It's been forever."

"My God, it feels like it," he says, kicking off the rest of his clothes, his cock standing at attention, tall and proud, announcing its intentions.

"Hello, there," I purr as I grasp his length, savoring the feel of it.

The bare, wonderful feel of him.

Which makes me take another chance.

I stare up at him. "West, I'm on birth control. And I've been tested, and the coast is clear, so…"

"Mmm. The coast is clear here too," he says, climbing on the bed, covering me with his body. As he does, I arch and shudder, all at the same time.

This man makes me feel everything all at once. Tenderness and desire. Friendship and swoony belly flips.

Joy and terror because we're no longer playing by my rules.

I thought I could set boundaries.

I thought I could have him just so. That he could be

the hot Englishman across the street, or the new friend I fuck.

Or maybe even an arrangement—Saturday night sex and Scrabble on Tuesday afternoons. No stress, no mess, no risk of losing big at the game of love.

But as West lavishes me in decadent kisses, it becomes increasingly clear that none of that would satisfy my hungry heart. It's a ravenous beast and it wants what it wants—West.

"Oh God, that feels so good. Everything just feels so good with you. *Everything*," I say, emphasizing that last word, hoping he knows I mean much more than his mouth.

He looks up from my belly then moves over my body to bestow greedy kisses on my lips. "Everything is incredible," he murmurs before he turns full bossy. "Now, part your legs for me. Spread them wide so I can fuck you deep and make love to you the way you want."

Hot tingles race down my body, settling between my legs, a desperate ache. "I want both," I whisper.

"So do I, darling. So do I."

I let my legs fall open for him, and he rubs the head of his cock against my wetness, nothing between us but skin and heat. It is delicious and his touch makes me delirious, absolutely *delirious* with want.

"Oh God, yes please," I beg.

"Hands above your head," he instructs, and I love that even like this, he still knows how to dominate, still knows I want it like that.

I follow his orders and arch into his touch, moaning as he pushes inside me then groaning like a wild thing when he sinks deeper. When he fills me all the way, my breath hitches, and my heart climbs the stairs.

"This is sooooo…"

"Sooo good," he finishes, savoring the intensity, too.

The connection.

The depth.

I want to throw my arms around his back and hold him close, bring him deep, but he already senses that. How I want it. How I crave him. He drives deeper, chest to chest, skin to skin, holding me close, his arms wrapped around my shoulders, his cock stroking deep inside me.

He thrusts, fucking me hard and beautifully. It feels like my body turns inside out with pleasure and my heart cracks wide open.

It's terrifying and perfect at the same time.

Terrifyingly perfect.

And when I break, splintering into thousands of beautiful pieces, he's right here with me, panting and groaning and saying my name like it matters.

Like I'm his.

GIGI

I've always craved a little bit of kink in the bedroom.

Hands tied.

Ass swatted.

Hair pulled.

After those first few years of teenaged fumbling when any kind of sex was new and exciting, I wasn't sure I would truly enjoy something as simple as basic missionary. And *that* kind of missionary. Bodies pressed together. Legs wrapped around his back. Necks and throats being kissed.

But I did.

Oh, holy hell, did I ever.

I enjoyed it everywhere, in every part of me.

And I want him to know.

After we transition to his fantastic claw-foot tub and I sink into the hot water between his legs, I turn to look at him. "I could get used to this," I say, even though nerves wind inside me.

Yes, fear is there, but strength and hope are calling the shots.

He presses a kiss to my hair. "Me too." I rest my head against his warm chest, wondering…

"Does that mean…" I begin.

"That we're seeing each other?" he supplies.

"Yes," I say with a smile.

"Well, it seems we already are. And have been. It seems we can't stay away from each other. Best to give into it all. Wouldn't you say?"

I'm giddy with hope, alive with possibilities. "I would say you're dating the competition."

He runs a finger down my chest, laughing. "Sleeping with the enemy."

"Dating the woman across the street," I toss back.

"Yes, it seems I'm quite mad about her."

I settle back into his chest with the happiest of sighs in all of Brooklyn.

No. Make that the entire city.

Especially when we eat peach pie in his bed after we get out of the tub.

Yes, I could get used to this.

* * *

Sometime in the middle of the night, I wake up to feel West wedged against me, his arm wrapped across my belly, his body warm but also hard.

I murmur as I push my butt against his erection. He murmurs too, a sleepy, sexy sound.

Then his fingers drift down my belly, between my legs, where he strokes me. "Already wet, love?"

"Already hard, love?" I ask, imitating him. He laughs, but then we both stop laughing when he pushes inside me and makes slow, sleepy love to me in the middle of the night, sending us both into sweet, dirty dreams once more.

Early the next morning, I grab fresh panties from my purse, tug them on, and twist up my hair. I stuff my dress into my gigantic handbag, pull on a pair of capri pants and a T-shirt, then I kiss a sleeping West goodbye.

He grabs my wrist. "Thank you for spending the night," he says, sounding so earnest and vulnerable.

"Thank you for asking me," I say, with a sashay of my hips. "Oh! You didn't ask me, I insisted."

"You ought to insist again." He presses a kiss to my hand.

"I will. I will insist away. And then I will beat your adorable ass tomorrow at the competition," I say, raising my chin.

"Like bloody hell you will."

I leave on that sassy note, practically bounding down the steps, out the door, and onto Church Street, where it feels like a brand-new day.

A brand-new start.

There's only one thing to do now…

I root around in my purse, grab my phone, and click open the thread with Ruby, tapping out a quick note. One that delights me to my very bones to send to her.

Gigi: You were right!

Ruby: Three of my favorite words. What was I right about?

Gigi: Oh God. I think he is the man of my dreams.
GIF of unicorn jumping over the rainbow
GIF of woman fainting and falling to the ground
GIF of cartoon cat fanning itself
GIF of Jason Segel clutching a pillow

Ruby: *GIF of smug-looking celebrity saying I told you so*
Okay now that you've sufficiently GIF-bombed me, tell me everything.

Gigi: We had the most incredible time and now we're DATING. Like two adults! We actually AGREED TO DATE. Not just be friends who boink like horny unicorns. Though we'll still do that, of course. But DATING! We're doing it!

Ruby: Dating as in that thing two people do when they stop playing games and decide they want to really give it a shot? And sometimes involves horny unicorns?

As I read her note, I tilt my head back, drinking in the sunshine and the blue sky, soaking in the perfection of this summer day. I glance around, taking in my neighborhood, enjoying all the sights, all the stores, everything I've loved my whole life.

Gigi: Yes. That thing. I'm told every now and then it can be wonderful.

Ruby: Yes. Yes, it can.

As I type a reply, I turn the corner to my street and smack right into a wall.

A wall of a man, with strong shoulders, sharp cheekbones, and swoopy Clark Kent hair.

His shoulder in my face hurts like hell.

"Ouch!" I rub my stinging nose.

But when I look up my stomach plummets.

"Nelson," I croak, in disbelief. "And Buttonista?"

My ex squints as if he's trying to place me. Then he snaps his fingers a few times. "Wait. Hold on. Don't tell me. You're…" His forehead smooths. "I helped you with your divorce from that jackass, right? A year or so ago?"

I sputter, searching for words. For a few brief seconds, righteous anger floods my cells before something truly unpleasant rushes in to replace it.

Shame. Mortification. And the primal fear that haunts me.

I'm not even memorable.

I dated him for three months and he can't remember my name, let alone the way I laugh, the way I fuck, the way I bought him little gifts too, so he'd know I was thinking of him when we were apart.

And now the brunette beauty next to him is beaming at me like we're about to be besties.

The woman extends a hand. "Gabriella. I just opened up a button shop in the neighborhood. My second location." Pride drips in her voice as she clutches Nelson's arm. "Isn't Nelson the best shark in the business? He got me out of my horrible marriage too. I'm so grateful to him." Then she lifts a finger in my direction. "We should grab a cup of tea and girl-talk sometime at that new tea place. We ladies have to stick together."

I stare at her, blinking, then at Nelson, trying to read him.

His face is stone.

I'm flummoxed, completely at a loss as to what's going on. Did he lie to Buttonista about being with me when he cheated with her? Is he expecting me to go along with his case of feigned amnesia? Or does he truly *not* remember me.

And in the grand scheme of things does it even matter?

Not really.

But my pride does.

I straighten my shoulders and draw a deep breath. "I'm not divorced. I've never been married. But I certainly hope, Gabriella, that you're happier now than you were before. And Nelson? Goodbye. *Again*."

I walk away with my dignity intact but tears streaming down my face. Once I'm a block away, they fall faster, stinging my skin.

Nelson was lying. Which is on him.

But there's something on me.

Something I'm responsible for.

My choices.

Do I have chronically awful taste in men?

And is West going to be the next guy I run into once

we're over, when he tires of me and finds another plaything who's more interesting than Gigi the curvy baker who loves dresses and her friends and nerdy games and has ordinary, pedestrian dreams like finding someone who wants to snuggle her for the rest of her life?

Back at my apartment, I rush inside, shut the door, and slump against the wall—feeling weirdly uncomfortable and unlovable all over again.

Deciding to indulge myself just this once, I call into Sweetie Pies that I won't be in today, after all, explaining I need time to plan my competition entry for tomorrow even though I've had it locked and loaded since the day after the first contest.

I am a very prepared person.

Just not a very memorable one.

Stop it, I insist as I change into a silk kimono and prop up in bed to watch old episodes of my favorite makeover show. *You* are *memorable and West isn't Awful Nasty Nelson.*

Nelson, who visibly cringed when I said something the tiniest bit nerdy or wanted to go to Trivia Night at the pub instead of martinis at whatever Manhattan hot spot he was desperate to be seen at. Nelson, who preferred for me to leave his place before midnight and never held me tight all night long.

My brain makes very good points here, but I'm still low for the rest of the day.

Even West's romantic text later that afternoon—*I'm dying for you to sleep over again, but tomorrow's opening day and Abby will kill me if I'm groggy because I was up all hours kissing every perfect inch of you*—can't banish the lingering gloom.

It makes me smile, but I'm not sad to have a good excuse to sleep in my own bed tonight.

I shoot back—*Abby is correct. And we both need rest for the contest tomorrow. But Saturday night? You're mine.*

All yours—he confirms.

For now, I think.

For now.

It's grand-opening day at the shop, and customers line up down the block. Abby, at the counter, and the two servers and busboy on duty in the dining area have all been slammed.

The madness is so intense that around eleven a.m. I call in another server and busboy, only for traffic to die down by the time they arrive.

But that's good.

Better too much help than too little. And Eli, the server, is fabulous in the kitchen.

I put him to work prepping the dough for tomorrow, when he and George, my second in command, will be in first to get the ovens going. Then I toss my dirty apron into the laundry bin and head out back for some fresh air.

There, I find Graham munching sandwiches in the garden. When he sees me, he lifts a pinkie finger.

"Hello," I say, laughing as I cross to clasp the hand he holds up in welcome. "You should have had your server tell me you were here. I would have sent out some extras with your order."

"I didn't want to bother you on your first day. Just wanted to provide friendly support and pick up scones for breakfast before I head home." He smiles his predatory businessman smile. "Sounds like that contest was as good for business as Abby hoped it would be. She said you were slammed all day."

I sink into the chair across from his with a satisfied sigh. "Yeah. We were."

"Made you even more determined to win it all? Leave those other chefs in the dust?"

I shrug and cross my arms, slumping a little lower. "Eh…"

"Eh?" He arches a brow. "What's that about? Don't tell me you're not enjoying the limelight."

"No, the limelight's fine. The first event was fun, and the buzz it generated was clearly brilliant, but…" I sigh again, a less satisfied one this time. "But I'm honestly considering dropping out."

Graham's brows shoot up. "What? You? But you're the most competitive person I know. You almost punched me over a poker game, for God's sake."

"You were cheating."

"We were playing for pennies!"

"I don't care. Cheating is cheating and it's a reprehensible thing to do no matter how big the pot." I drag a hand down my face. "But that's different. I like to win, yes, but I like…other things more."

Graham tosses the last of his rosemary and goat cheese sandwich onto his plate. "This is about a woman, isn't it? Specifically, that chef from game night you tied with in the first round."

"Gigi." I lean forward, propping my elbows on the table. "She just wants it so much more than I do. And dammit, I *want* her to have it, even if it upsets Abby." I wince. "I'm a terrible brother."

Graham laughs. "You *are* a terrible brother. And apparently a huge softie when you're in love."

"Shut up." I snort and grin, waving him off. "I just met her. No one falls in love that fast."

He nods. "Yeah. There's probably some other perfectly logical explanation for you wanting to put her dreams first. And the way your face gets all moony when you say her name."

I narrow my eyes. "Smug isn't a good look for you, in case you're wondering."

"It's a great look, I'm positive. I'm enjoying this so much." He laughs again, relishing my suffering.

That's what I've been doing since Gigi left my place yesterday—suffering.

I can't stop thinking about her, and not just in an I-want-her-back-in-my-bed-ASAP sort of way, either.

I want to hear her voice, know what she's thinking. I want to see her smile and hear her laugh. I want to see what flirty little thing she's wearing, and I'm absolutely looking forward to being the man who gets to take it off her when the day is through.

And I want to do whatever it takes to make her happy, even if it means disappointing my sister and going against my fiercely competitive instincts.

And I fucking know what that means.

I *know*, even before Graham says, "Here's the thing I've learned from falling for my best friend. Love doesn't always adhere to your preconceived notions."

"But there are still tons of things I don't know about her," I say, though the argument feels flimsy. "Like, what kind of music she likes. Or if she's ever been to Paris."

Graham rolls his eyes. "Right. Because no love ever survived a difference in musical tastes, or one person having seen the Eiffel Tower and not the other."

"The tower is the least exciting part of Paris," I grunt and slump lower in my chair.

He drops his voice to a stage whisper. "True. But also, if she says she likes Matt Nathanson tunes, just tell her to put him on. He's catnip for women."

"Always classy, you are."

He smirks. "And so are you."

I motion for him to keep talking. "Go on, wise old married man with your musical advice. Convince me I might be mad for this amazing, sexy, utterly delightful woman at this scandalously early date."

He grins at the description. I acknowledge his smirk with an eye roll. And he asks, "Can you talk to her? Really talk?"

"Yes," I say without hesitation.

"And she listens?"

"Fabulously."

"Is she nice to waiters?"

"Very. She's nice to everyone. Except me, of course, when she thought I was a dirty liar who'd tricked her into letting down her guard, but once I explained things, she wasn't stingy with her forgiveness."

Graham claps his hands together. "There you have it. All you need to know."

I wrestle with disbelief before I can reply. "Fine, I concede I'm falling for the woman, but what kind of crap advice is that, Graham? 'Can we talk?' and, 'Is she nice to waiters?'" I snort. "I'm sizing up a major commitment for fuck's sake, not hiring a new book-keeper. Though, she'd be amazing at that," I admit. "She's wild with numbers. and it's sexy as hell."

Graham frowns. "Okay, numbers can be sexy, but my advice isn't crap. The sex is amazing, or you wouldn't be in deep this fast. And, being practical, the two of you have more than a few shared interests." He ticks off on his fingers. "Great sex, common interests, and solid conversation with a woman who's as kind to the people serving her tea as she'd be to a friend. What more do you need in a life partner?"

Life partner...

That phrase would usually make me gag a little. Or, at the very least, make me take a moment to reflect that my history with relationships isn't great. I probably shouldn't rush into anything. Lessons learned and all.

But Gigi would be an amazing partner. And spending a hell of a lot more time with her—maybe even a lifetime—isn't a scary thought.

It's more like the first sip of a perfectly cream-and-honeyed cup of Lapsang souchong, a tempting treat that makes me eager for more.

"Not to mention that she's insanely gorgeous," Graham says, taking a sip of his tea.

I look up fast. "What? You saw her? When? When we were leaving the party?"

"No, outside. Maybe twenty minutes ago." He motions toward the street. "She and Abby were chatting on the corner by the shoe store before I came in. They looked friendly."

I jump to my feet then immediately sit back down. "I can't force my sister to tell me everything Gigi said to her and then announce I'm dropping out of the competition. That would be madness."

Graham chuckles. "Maybe not madness, but very middle school."

I drag a hand through my hair, fighting temptation for another hot second before I say, "Be right back," and bolt through the door into the shop, across the indoor seating area, and behind the counter.

There, Abby is ringing up a man in a pork pie hat that instantly makes me think of Gigi—the woman has invaded every damn corner of my mind. And I love it. I truly do.

I force myself to let Abby finish the transaction. But the man has scarcely turned away before I'm beside her, demanding, "Gigi. What did she say to you? Tell me everything."

Abby grins up at me and winks. "Wouldn't you like to know."

"I love you dearly. So don't make me strangle it out of you. I'd like to move forward without marring our sibling bond."

She giggles and reaches beneath the counter, pulling out a small wooden jewelry box. "She just wanted to welcome me to the neighborhood. She gave me a gift certificate for the super cute shoe store on the corner and this. For you."

I take the box reverently. "For me?"

"Yeah, open it," she says, making shooing motions with her hands. "I'm dying of curiosity. She was so cute when she handed it over."

"Cute?" I turn the box over, but nothing shifts inside. "In what way? Aside from the obvious, of course."

"A little shy, a little flushed." Abby bobs her brows as she adds in a singsong, "I think someone might have a crush on my big brother."

"No, she doesn't," I say in a tone that gives away how much I'd like for that—and something much more serious than that—to be true.

A tone that doesn't escape my sister's notice.

"Aw, and you have a crush, too! Perfect. You're going to make delicious babies together." She sighs happily. "Just stunning little creatures. No doubt in my mind. I'm excited already. I call dibs on hosting the first baby shower. You should have three. Or four. Babies, not showers."

Before I can tell her to stop being ridiculous and give me the goods already, a woman pushes through the front door and steps up to the counter. "Do you still have raspberry scones? I tried some of my girlfriend's after yoga, and I'm dying for at least six more."

While Abby makes our customer's scone dreams come true, I open my present, creaking open the lid to reveal a fine pair of cufflinks. They're small and a bit tarnished—must be antique—and in the shape of tiny teacups complete with a teabag string dangling down the side. A note folded into the top of the box reads— *The scared part of me said not to buy these or to let you know how often you're on my mind. But the hopeful part said these were made for you and you simply must wear them to the competition today. And that it's okay to let you know that I think of you warmly and fondly...and often with wet panties. ;) Good luck today. You're going to need it, boyfriend! xo–Gigi*

"Damn," I mutter, my throat tight and my chest...warm.

Very warm.

I'm in deep fucking trouble.

I don't want to compete with this woman. I want to cheer her on and buy her a beautiful meal to celebrate her victory. And maybe some really expensive jewelry because she'd be stunning in a sapphire necklace the same color as her eyes.

And nothing else.

"I'm going to break your heart," I tell Abby as she returns to my side, trusting the knot in my gut that says this competition isn't for me. Not anymore. "I'm so sorry."

Abby leans against the counter and props a hand on her fist. "Okay, break away."

"I'm serious," I insist.

She laughs. "No, you're not. You would never, could never break my heart. You're my big brother, the best person I know, and secretly a big squishy teddy bear."

I frown. "You're the second person to say something like that today. I'm not squishy. I'm fierce and determined and brave enough to tell you that," I stop to draw a fueling breath, "I'm going to drop out of the competition."

Abby makes a "huh" sound but doesn't look all that surprised. "All right. But Gigi won't want you to. She'll want to beat you. If you drop out, you'll deprive her of that pleasure."

I frown harder. "You're wrong. She wants to win, and she'll have a better chance of that if I'm out of the running."

"She wants to win *and* beat you and then spend all night kissing it better at your place to heal your wounded man-pride. Trust me. I have good instincts about things like this. She got a spark in her eye when she talked about the contest. Reminded me of you."

I pause, pondering her words. "I guess we are similar in that way."

"You guess?" She laughs. "And how would you feel if she dropped out to clear your path to victory."

I scowl again. "Awful. I'd rather lose to her fair and square."

Abby tips her head. "And there you go. But you could make her the offer, just to be sure. And then you two should find something to be fiercely competitive about together. You'll have more fun if you're on the same team."

The same team. With Gigi.

It sounds like the way I want to end every day and wake up every morning.

"I'm going to head out a little earlier than planned," I say. "Is that all right?"

"Of course. I told you to leave earlier. Sometimes the trains to Coney Island are slow on Fridays, and you don't want to be late for the competition."

"No, I don't," I murmur, heading for the door only to spin around and head back to the garden to say goodbye to my friend.

But Graham is already on his way through the dining area to the counter and waves me off. "Go. Profess your love. I'll touch base later. And good luck, whatever you decide."

I lift a hand to him, and then to Abby, indicating that she should give Graham whatever he wants at no charge, and then I leave before he can start a fight about it.

I have too much to get done before four o'clock to waste even a second. I have a woman to woo and charm and convince that the hopeful part of her is my favorite part.

Because I'm hopeful too, and I aim to prove it.

GIGI

I step out of the subway at the Coney Island stop and make my way down the ramp. My heart is pounding restlessly even before a homeless woman in a prom dress nearly mows me down with her shopping cart by the entrance to the boardwalk.

I'm losing my cool. All of it.

And *not* because it's eighty-five degrees and I'm starting to have serious concerns about my ice cream treat surviving long enough to be judged in this heat.

No, I'm nervous because instead of retreating to safer ground I went and crawled out onto an even skinnier, spindlier limb.

Those antique teacup cufflinks at the local flea market I visited during my lunch break were too perfect for West *not* to be purchased. One does not simply ignore a gift from the shopping gods. But I could have bought them and set them aside for a later date or a special occasion. I didn't have to immediately gift them to him with a brutally honest note about My Feelings.

And yes, I bought a cover present for his sister too, but I'm not fooling anyone. Not myself. And not West, I'm sure.

He's very smart. It's one of the things I like best about him, in fact. His big sexy brain. And I'm sure that big sexy brain of his knows exactly what a big deal that present and that note are for me.

And surely, he's received both by now.

Abby promised to give them to him before he left for the competition.

But it's been a while.

I check my phone as I wander down the crowded boardwalk toward the Mr. or Mrs. Sweet Stuff tent, this time set up by the carousel beside the beach.

Yep, nearly three hours since I made the drop. And I haven't heard from West. Not a call or a text or so much as a sparkly-eyed emoji to communicate his feelings about my feelings.

I tell myself he was slammed at the shop and then probably rushing around to get ready for the contest and just hasn't had the chance to text.

But I'm still nervous.

Fidgety.

So on edge that when a low voice purrs behind me, "Excuse me, are these ears taken?" I jump several inches in the air and let out a squeal that makes everyone in front of me turn to stare.

I wave at the concerned Coney Island citizens—tourists, clearly, judging by the gaudy T-shirts and the hands full of hot dogs and overpriced cotton candy—and turn to West.

"You can't sneak up on me," I say with a laugh as I swat at the general vicinity of his stomach. "I'm high strung before battle."

"Sorry." He looks gorgeous in a white button-down, navy tie, and a gray suit vest and pants with his cooking bag slung over his shoulder.

I can't resist the urge to reach out and tweak his collar. "You look amazing."

"Same to you, gorgeous." His gaze gobbles me up in a way that makes me *feel* gorgeous—and silly for being nervous. Clearly West is every bit as happy to see me as I am to see him. He holds out his wrist with a grin. "Thank you for the gift. They're perfect."

I glance down, taking his hand in mine and spinning the little teacup cufflink with a satisfied sigh. "They are. If I do say so myself. Which I do."

"And you should." He reaches into his pocket with his free hand. "I was so touched that I had to get you a little something in return."

Beaming, I accept the medium-sized blue velvet jewelry box. "Oh, you didn't have to. I love giving gifts, but I never expect anything in return."

"Of course you don't, because you're lovely, inside and out," he says, making my heart squeeze and my throat a little tight.

God, it feels like I've been waiting my whole life to hear that. And to see someone look at me like I'm the best gift he's ever found under his Christmas tree or anywhere else.

"But it's high time someone spoiled you the way you deserve," he continues, nodding toward the box. "We'll start with this and carry on with the spoiling after the contest. Assuming you're free and interested in spending some time with your boyfriend?"

Ohhh.

Well, hello there, yummy word.

It's exactly what I want. Precisely what I was hoping for, but I hardly dared to let myself believe he'd be ready for that so soon.

But he is, and I am giddy with happiness from one perfect word that sums up what he is to me.

I grin harder. "The answer to both is yes." I lower my voice and add with more confidence than I feel, "And don't tell anyone, but I feel very fizzy inside when you talk about being my boyfriend."

He laughs. "Good. Now open it, woman, the suspense is killing me."

"Okay." I creak open the box, expecting something sweet and pie-themed in keeping with my gift. Instead, I reveal a pair of tasteful but clearly insanely fucking expensive sapphire and diamond chandelier earrings. My jaw drops. "Those aren't...real. Are they?" I ask, though my sparkly-sense has never failed me before.

"Of course, they are," he scoffs. "I'm not going to buy you rot-gut jewelry that'll turn your lovely ears green." He reaches into his bag. "Try them on. And if you decide you'd rather return them for something else, that's completely fine."

My jaw fully unhinges, but I finally manage to stammer as I slip the earrings in, "Shut your face. I'm not taking them back. I may never take them *off*. They're the most beautiful thing I've ever seen."

"Nah," he says, though he's clearly pleased as he grabs his phone from his pocket, turns it to selfie mode, and holds it up in front of me. The makeshift mirror gives me an up-close-and-personal view of the stunning jewelry. He seems even more delighted with the way I melt when he adds, "You're the most beautiful. But the stones do match your eyes. I hoped they would."

The line should sound cheesy, I suppose. But the way he says it—so offhand, like he's simply announcing a commonly known fact—makes me want to laugh and cry and kiss him all at the same time.

I decide kissing is the best call and jump into his arms, making him laugh as he tries to juggle his bag, his phone, and me all at once.

But he manages. Of course, he does.

He's West and he's amazing.

And he's mine.

For real, *mine*, and he seems to like me just as I am. Or…even better, the way I've always wanted to be if I weren't so gun-shy when it comes to relationships.

"I love them so much," I say as I kiss his cheek, leaving a lipstick mark behind. "Love, love, love."

"I'm so glad," he says as he sets me back on my feet. "I was looking for a necklace, but they didn't have any that were just right. I'm a picky bastard when it comes to jewelry."

A part of me wants to stress about how many women he's bought jewelry for before me, but I ignore that voice. I don't have to be jealous of the women from his past. Because I'm his present, and maybe his future.

I reach up to cup his face and sigh. "This is going to

make it much harder to relish crushing you beneath my high-heeled Mary Janes in round two."

"Yeah, about that," he says, and then his mouth keeps moving and he says things that are so wonderfully generous and sweet that for a moment I'm struck full force by an insane thought—*He loves me. Like, really loves me*—but thankfully I realize how crazy that is before I say something stupid.

He just isn't as serious about cooking or this competition as I am.

Or…something.

Or maybe his competitive streak is taking a day off.

Whatever it is, I hurry to assure him, "No way! Stop it. I wouldn't dream of asking you to drop out."

"You're not asking. I'm offering," he says. "And I truly don't mind, either way. It's your call. I just wanted you to know the offer was on the table, if you think it might help you win." He clears his throat and looks around, before leaning in to add in a faux confidential voice of his own, "I'm pretty keen to date the next Mrs. Sweets. It's a status thing. Make my friends wickedly jealous."

I grin and tease, "You'll still get to date her. You'll just have to get beaten by her first." I take his hand. "Come on. No dropping out. We're in this to the end. Or until my ice cream melts into a puddle and I'm disqualified."

He groans as we start toward the tent, hand in hand. "Fucking hot as balls out here. I don't know what they expect us to do in this weather. Hard to achieve culinary brilliance with the heat and the wind blowing sand into everything and tourists tracking hypodermic needles into the tent." He wrinkles his nose at the beach. "I actually tried to walk across the sand the first time I was here. Won't make that mistake again. It's a bloody hazardous waste dump out there."

I laugh. "Oh, but it's so much better than it used to be. You have no idea. It used to be super dirty. Scary, too."

As we stroll, I regale him with stories of the creepy Coney Island freak show my dad took my brother and me to when I was seven. "Harrison had to lead me through it like a blind person," I add, "because I was too terrified to open my eyes."

"Good brother," West observes. "I'd like to meet him. Since you've already completely seduced my sister, I figure I should start getting on your brother's good side sometime soon."

I nod and squeeze his hand a little tighter. "You should. It'll be easy. He'll like you." I grin. "So, Abby likes me, huh?"

"Love at first sight," he says. "You'd better watch out or—" He breaks off with a glare as we near the tent. "What is that wretched man up to now?"

I follow his gaze to see Hawley in a yellow polo shirt crouched beneath one of the cook stations, taking the bottom off one of the ice-cream makers with a screwdriver.

Before I can warn West that we should go to one of the organizers instead of calling out another contestant for potential foul play, West is jogging across the wooden pier and into the tent, clearly ready to rumble.

I can count the times I've hit a man on one hand.

On two fingers, in fact.

Once when I was on holiday in Greece and some drunk wanker thought I'd touched his girlfriend's arse —I hadn't—and threw the first punch.

I threw the next, he stumbled over on the sand and stayed there, and that was that.

The second time was at a bachelor party. The bachelor, a poorly chosen friend from my investment banking days, got handsy with the stripper and punched me when I tried to intervene. I gave him a black eye that ruined the wedding photos the next day.

Or so I was told.

I was *un*invited after I wrapped the stripper in my coat and gave her a ride to her flat.

I'm not a violent man and have *never* thrown the first punch, but for some reason, I desperately want to hit Hawley. And not just because he's apparently fucking with the equipment in an attempt to cheat his way to the top.

No, it's because of Gigi.

Of what she said the other night.

You should be more kind and careful with a lover than a friend.

She's so fucking right. And instead of being kind or careful with my sister, this man made Abby feel like she's a fool who doesn't deserve to be treasured or adored. And yes, Hawley's been a piece of shit for a while now, but the way I feel for Gigi brings home in a new way just how nightmarish it is to accept a woman's trust and then violate it so brutally.

And the fact that he did that to my sweet, smart, lovely sister...

Smash.

I want to smash his face and worry about the consequences later.

Thankfully, Willow pops into my line of sight before I can do anything rash.

"Hey, West," she says with an only slightly shy smile. "I saw the crowd outside your place this morning. Congratulations on the amazing opening!"

"Thank you." I divide my attention between Hawley, who's now placing the device he was tampering with on the countertop in front of him, and Willow, in front of me. "It was a wonderful surprise. My sister was very excited. And relieved. She's been more worried about the bottom line."

"That's great, though, to have someone focused on

that," Willow says, pushing her glasses up her nose. "I wish I had a money person. And I wish it wasn't so hot."

"Boiling," Gigi agrees as she joins us, hooking her arm through my elbow and shooting a curious look up at me that asks *Are you okay?*

I sigh. "I'm fine. Willow saved me from myself." Willow frowns and I explain, "I was on my way to punch Hawley. Or perhaps something slightly less violent, but still inappropriate."

"It seemed like he was tampering with some of the equipment," Gigi explains. "But it looks like it's for his station, so…"

Willow glances over her shoulder and turns back with a thoughtful expression. "Yes, that is his station. He borrowed a screwdriver from one of the organizers so he could slow down the churn speed on his machine. He's doing a custard."

Gigi pats my arm. "See there. It's all good."

"Well…" Willow tugs a lock of her hair.

"Well?" I prompt. "Has he been bothering you? If so, that face-smashing offer is still on the table."

She shakes her head. "No, I was just…thinking about the fire at the last event. That hot plate that caught my apron wasn't plugged in when I got to my station. I know because I checked to make sure I'd have enough room for my mixer *and* my submersion blender, and nothing else was plugged in. So maybe someone else plugged it in? And I'm not sure, but I think Hawley was the only other person who was ever behind the counter at my station. He was walking around—"

"Sticking his nose into everyone's business," I finish with a nod. "I saw that too. And I wouldn't put sabotage past him. His moral fiber is about as firm as a cookie dunked in milk one too many times."

Gigi hums beneath her breath. "Or graham crackers. They really do fall to pieces in a cup of milk."

I glance down at her, a smile breaking across my face at the sight of my earrings glittering against her red curls. Even when I'm in the mood to smash faces, she just gets to me. She's so damn adorable and beautiful and correct about graham crackers.

I tell her so, then add to Willow, "So be sure to check your station closely and don't leave it unattended after you do. And Gigi and I have your back, of course."

"Absolutely," Gigi agrees.

"But if he did do that...why me?" Willow wonders, her brow furrowing as she fans her flushed face. "I'm not much of a threat."

Gigi wags a finger her way. "Stop it. You came in second last time, woman! You're a talent and a force to be reckoned with. If I were into winning via foul play, I'd totally sneak salt into your sugar canister."

Willow smiles, but it's almost immediately replaced by a grimace. "I'm going to go check my sugar and salt right now. Just in case."

"Good thinking," I say. "And good luck." As she scurries off, I turn to Gigi and whisper, "Last chance to tell me to stand down. Speak now, or don't be sad when my melted ice cream disaster is slightly less awful than your melted ice cream disaster."

She grins and tips her head back. "Never. Hit me with your best shot, buddy, and I'll see you after the judging."

"See you soon," I murmur, watching her move to meet the staff member approaching through the shaded tent.

For a moment, I dare to hope it might be cool enough in the shade to make a difference, but as my own helpful staff member shows me to my station, it becomes clear it's actually *more* stifling under here. The flap on one side of the tent blocks the sea breeze—good for keeping sand out of our sweets, but bad for air flow.

Very bad.

By the time Mr. Skips has welcomed the onlookers and explained we'll each have forty minutes to create our ice-cream inspired offering, the back of my shirt is sticking to my skin and I know modifications must be made. Removing my cufflinks and tucking them into my pants pocket, I roll up my sleeves and remove my vest, draping it over the stool at the back of my station.

I turn back to the shelves below my counter.

That's when I see the red ice cream machine tucked behind the silver one on the top shelf. If I weren't a good three feet away, I wouldn't have noticed the second one, I'm sure. I would have snatched up the silver and gotten down to business. It's going to take at least twenty-five minutes for the ice cream to freeze in the machine, after all, so there's no time to waste getting my recipe assembled. And who would imagine there was more than one maker on offer?

Glancing around the stations as the other contestants set to work, I see that almost everyone seems to have a red or blue machine. No silver. And on the shelves in my line of sight, it appears each chef has only one maker to choose from.

Huh...

I crouch to arrange the machines side by side and glace quickly at the specs for each. The silver one is an older model and requires a pre-frozen bowl—a bowl that is presently sitting *in* the machine in the sweltering heat, nowhere close to frozen. If I'd put my base in there, I would have had a lightly chilled soup forty-five minutes later, not anything close to ice cream.

If I didn't know better, I'd think...

But, of course, I *do* know better. And I *do* think.

I stand with the red machine in hand, casting a narrow-eyed glare Hawley's way as I plug it in. But the bastard isn't looking at me. He's pouring cream into a saucepan, an innocently focused look on his face.

Too innocent and too focused.

But I don't have enough time or evidence to call him out for attempted sabotage right now. Though, of course, it *had* to be him. The rest of these contestants actually have a shred or two of integrity.

After a quick check to make sure Gigi and Willow both have the right sort of machines—they seem to—I set to work.

I'm bringing my London Fog ice cream base to a simmer—heavy whipping cream, sweetened condensed milk, Earl Grey tea, and my signature blend of spices—when Gigi clears her throat. Loudly.

I look up, sensing the sound is meant for me.

Our eyes meet across the counter of the cook station between us, currently occupied by an older woman I didn't have the chance to meet last time. Gigi casts a wide-eyed glance at the counter behind me, where my ice cream maker is starting to smoke.

Gently.

And then, not so gently.

Lunging across the small space, I jerk the plug from the socket, earning myself an unpleasant shock in the process.

Cursing beneath my breath, I lift a hand to one of the staff members gliding up and down the aisles. I explain the situation with the malfunctioning machine and the unsuitable machine still on the shelf, and the helpful young chap rushes off to secure me another.

I set to work on my lavender sugar cookie batter, knowing the cookies have to be in the oven in five minutes if they're going to cool enough to top the ice cream.

I've just barely plunked the ingredients in the standing mixer, however, when the staff member returns with Mr. Skips.

For once, the cheery elf looks fretful.

"I'm so sorry, but we don't have a spare machine," he says softly. "I would have sworn we had extras in the truck, but I just looked, and the bin is empty."

I exhale and bite my lip, propping my hands on my hips as I try to sort out a solution.

"He can have mine," Gigi calls out. I turn to see her swiftly mixing something in a silver bowl as she nods toward her machine. "Mine is coming out in ten minutes. I'll pop it in the freezer and give the bowl a quick rinse. That should give West time to get his ice cream through, too."

"Brilliant." Mr. Skips's apple cheeks pop as his familiar grin returns. "I'll stay close and facilitate the cleaning and transition of the equipment. Thank you, Miss James."

"Of course!" Gigi beams a smile at both of us, then adds a quick wink for me, and turns back to her work, having seamlessly offered a helping hand while fiercely pursuing her own goals.

I fucking love that about her.

As if reading my mind, Mr. Skips adds beneath his breath, "She's lovely. I've known her since she was a little girl. Sweetest soul you'll ever meet."

"Agreed," I murmur, my ribs giving my heart a squeeze.

And then, even though winning this contest isn't high on my list at the moment, I turn back to my work and give it my all too.

Because that's what my Gigi wants, and damn it, I intend to give her what she wants.

Everything she wants.

I can't wait to figure out what that is. Some things I already know, of course—good food, great kinky sex, lots of laughter, and integrity and tenacity in all games of skill and chance—but there's still so much to learn.

I want to discover every facet of Gigi. I want to read her like a good book—quickly the first time through because it's too exciting to take my time and then slower the second and third times, savoring every beautiful sentence and perfectly executed plot twist.

There are only a handful of books I've read more than once. And I have a feeling she's the *only* woman I'll ever want to know this way.

25

GIGI

This time, I'm only sweating from the heat.

Not from being judged.

I certainly don't love being judged, but I'm handling it better. A few days of putting myself out there with West is working wonders to soothe my anxiety prickles.

Turns out sharing My Feelings has some welcome side effects.

A smidge more courage.

A touch more gumption.

I stand tall, waiting as Mr. Skips clears his throat, cups his hand around his mouth as a megaphone for the cooking competition crowd. "What a delicious day for ice cream lovers! With those fantastic concoctions, we're a few cups and cones closer to learning who'll take home the prize. Before I announce the winners of this round, a brief reminder—the contestant with the most points at the conclusion of the final event wins. And now, in third place with eight points is Willow Thompson."

I turn to the sweet and clever woman who's becoming my friend and give her a silent *yay*. She smiles back, big and genuine, her cheeks flushed behind her red-framed-glasses.

"In second place, West Byron and Frederick James Ebenezer Hawley with eight and a half points each," Mr. Skips says.

My heart slams to the ground.

Crushed like a cigarette butt beneath a boot on the Coney Island beach.

That means I didn't even make the top three. I'm not going to stand a chance at being Mrs. Sweets.

I wince but lift my chin, saying strong.

Mr. Skips chuckles, a cheery sound, as he reads the final name. "And the winner of the round, with nine points, is Gigi James and her peach cobbler and goat cheese ice cream masterpiece. Congratulations, Gigi! Innovative and incredible work," he says with a *go-get-em-girl* pump of his fist.

Wow. I did not expect that.

At all.

Glee rushes through me, along with a tingly sense that victory is in my grasp.

I've always loved games and challenges, competitions of any kind really, but I'd really love to lock this title down. For my family's business. For what it can do for Sweetie Pies. And for what it says about me—that I can carry on the family legacy just fine.

The trouble is, victory is sweetest when it comes fair and square. And today's triumph most decidedly did *not*.

Hawley doesn't deserve second place. His stunt was

total poppycock. No, I can't prove he's the one who sabotaged West's machine, but I overheard some of the staff whispering while I was putting the finishing touches on my dish. Apparently, one of them spotted Hawley earlier coming out of the equipment truck with a duffle bag. If he wasn't snatching the extra ice cream makers—after messing with West's to make sure it wouldn't work—I'll drink an entire pot of tea without cream or sugar.

I didn't call Nelson on his bullshit yesterday—and I stand by that choice—but that guy over there in the aqua shorts and a pastel yellow polo shirt? His hood-winkery today?

Unacceptable.

He messed with my man. He damaged my boyfriend's chances to win this thing. West might not care about the contest. But I do. And contests need to be won by playing by the rules.

I take off my earrings, set them in my purse, and march over to the prick in pastel, plastering a smile on my face. The best way to begin any confrontation? Kill them with kindness.

"Congratulations," I coo. "You're doing so well. And I wanted to tell you, I recently had one of your fabulous frozen eclairs. Absolutely delicious," I tell him, wishing it were a lie, hating that it's not.

The man does make tremendous treats.

Which only makes his cheating more unforgivable. It's not like he needs an edge.

"Ah, thank you so much. You're a doll." His lips curve into a smug, entitled grin. "And so talented. I've actually been thinking of adding frozen pies to my product line. Maybe we could go into business together. What do you think? Would you consider letting me commission a few of your recipes?" he asks, throwing me for a loop.

For a split second, I'm flattered.

And a little tempted.

The man *does* run a food empire.

Yes, Sweetie Pies does very well with direct orders on our website, but our pies aren't in grocery stores.

For several tantalizing seconds, I imagine my pies in his distribution network and how exciting it would be to see my recipes in the freezer section.

But then I picture West's smoking ice cream maker, and I burn inside.

I am passionate about a lot of things, including my boyfriend.

I give a polite, yet crusty, "Thank you so much. But they're family recipes. They're not for sale, though I appreciate your interest." I smile. "Speaking of interest, I'm sooo curious. What, exactly, were you doing in the equipment truck earlier?"

He blinks. "Excuse me?"

"The truck. One of the staff members saw you coming out with a duffle bag."

He smiles, a sickly false one. "They must be mistaken. I've been here in the tent since I arrived."

"Huh. Really?" I press. "Seems hard to imagine there are that many men around wearing such nicely starched pastel."

His eyes narrow. "We're beachside. Pastel is a natural choice."

"Is it?" I narrow my eyes back at him. "Look around and find one other person in that crowd wearing anything close to what you're wearing. Go ahead. I'll wait."

His lips curve in a meaner, harder smile. "As amusing as this conversation is, I've reached my limit on indulging paranoia today, buttercup."

Oh no he didn't.

He did *not* say that.

The kid gloves are coming off.

I park my hands on my hips. "One, I am not a buttercup. You don't get to give me a nickname. Especially, a diminutive one. Two, it's not paranoia. You committed ice cream subterfuge and you know it."

He cackles, tossing his head back, his perfectly styled hair not even moving. Not a single hair. "Ice cream subterfuge? What next? Candy sabotage? Chocolate chicanery? Do you even hear yourself?"

I resist the urge to back down in the face of his scorn. People like him use shame as a weapon and I refuse to let Captain Buttercup land a blow.

"Ridiculous. I agree. But that's what you were doing," I say, mincing no words. "And you were messing with my boyfriend. You were trying to knock him out of the running."

His brow pinches. "Your boyfriend? How interesting. How very interesting," he murmurs. "Well, I hope you two enjoy exchanging kisses over paranoid conspiracy theories. Perhaps name your next ice cream flavor...*subterfuge*."

"Perhaps I will." I lean closer and whisper sweetly,

"Also, you're kind of a twat. And by 'kind of,' I mean you are definitely a twat."

I spin on my heel and walk away.

I'm not a hater. But man, it felt incredibly good to tell off that frozen-food, easter-egg-impersonating prick.

I meet West at his station as he's gathering the last of his things. He arches a brow at me before glancing over my shoulder at Hawley. "I trust whatever that was went well?"

"Yep. Tell you all about it on our date," I say with a grin. "I assume we're going on a date?"

"Hell, yes, we are. Right this very second."

* * *

The stars don't twinkle at night in New York City, but I swear I can feel them sparkling overhead in the inky velvet sky. It's that kind of night—a night for starlight and kisses, for holding hands and whispering sweet *everythings*.

West drapes an arm around me as we wander through the crowds at the Luna Park amusement park by the beach. "Tell me one more time," he says, his delight clear in his voice. "What did he do when you called him a twat?"

"He did this." I pull a crinkly, slack-jawed face as we make our way to the Ferris wheel.

He laughs. "Brilliant. Absolutely brilliant. I might need you to tell me that story again before bed."

I rest my head against his shoulder briefly. "And I'll happily do it."

Ah, bed. We'll be heading there soon. Together.

Happy sigh.

We reach the Ferris wheel and stand in line. As we wait, we are *that* couple. The one everyone wants to be. Holding hands, touching hair, laughing. As we amble closer, we talk about our favorite bands and singers.

I learn he loves Radiohead and Rush, two bands I can't stand, though their music is slightly less disgusting than beets and turnips, an opinion I share with West that makes him laugh again, since it turns out he detests those veggies too. I tell him that I adore Broadway musicals and the swooniest of male singers like Matt Nathanson and Harry Connick Jr. "I also love Sam Smith," I confess.

"Then I'll play a Sam Smith tune the next time I seduce you," he whispers as we walk up the ramp, closer to the entrance of the ride.

I tip my face closer to his. "I'm gonna let you in on a little secret. You've already seduced me. Big time."

"Very good to hear, but seducing isn't something you check off a list and consider it done, Gigi. It's a calling of the highest, most noble order to keep seducing your beautiful, sexy woman day after day."

Swoon.

He's doing it.

He is absolutely doing it—seducing me over and over.

The young, tattooed ride attendant clears his throat.

"Step right up. No rocking. No troublemaking. And please don't spit."

I wrinkle my nose.

As we head to the cage, I shoot West a curious look. "Was that really necessary? Do people do that? Spit at the top of Ferris wheels?"

"Seems they do. If you're interested, I'm up for breaking the rules. But fair warning, I'm an excellent spitter. Two older brothers and all."

"Gross," I say pleasantly as I run my hand along his arm then squeeze his bicep. "I had no idea this icky, boyish side of you existed. But I kind of like it."

"Brilliant. But let's hold off on the belching contest. I need a pint or two to really perform in that arena."

"If you insist." I laugh.

"I do insist. From the bottom of my big bossy heart."

I tap his sternum, then run my hand over his chest. "It is very big and very bossy."

"Just the way you like it."

"Guilty," I say as we settle into the seat, rocking back and forth as the Ferris wheel starts to climb.

He clasps my hand, brings my palm to his lips, kisses me. "Tell me something I don't know about you. Have you ever been to Europe?"

I sigh. "I haven't. It's a travesty, but I've always been too busy with work. But I would love to see Big Ben and the Eiffel Tower, and I definitely want to go all the way to the top, and I don't care if that's cheesy." I cut a glance his way. "I bet you hate the Eiffel Tower."

He smiles and confirms, "It's my least favorite part of

Paris. But I'll happily take you to the top and stay there as long as you like."

I harrumph. "Fine. What's your favorite part of Paris?"

As the Ferris wheel circles higher, he runs his fingers through my hair, his gaze holding mine. His dark eyes shine with desire, but something deeper, too. Something that feels powerful and real and like it's not stupid to imagine seeing Paris with him.

Seeing the world with him.

Maybe even my next ten or twenty birthdays with him.

"My favorite part of Paris is taking you for a visit at your earliest convenience," he whispers, and I'm done for.

That's it. I'm waving the white flag. Throwing in the towel.

I am head over heels in love with this man. It's only been six days, but I don't care. He's the man of my dreams. And it's time for me to tell him so. To take the first step.

To put my heart on the line.

Because I feel it.

And most of all because it's true to the better, brighter version of myself I'm becoming.

Less afraid. More daring.

But still, this is so damn hard. I do my best to swallow down the nerves and the giddy butterflies, except they're fluttering inside me in equal measure. I run my thumb along his jaw, then cup his cheek. "West Byron, magnificent spitter, wonderful human, person I am so glad I met over a Rubik's Cube… I am falling madly in love with you."

His smile is melting chocolate. "What do you know? I'm falling madly in love with you too, Gigi James." Then he kisses me just as we reach the top of the Ferris wheel, with all of Brooklyn spread out below and the stars sparkling just for us, even if we can't see them.

As we kiss, the Coney Island firework show begins.

It is a perfect night.

Wait. No.

It's even better. It's *just so*.

26

WEST

The next week is the best week. Ever.

Life is fucking beautiful and I'm fucking in love and fucking the most amazing woman in the world and if I weren't already running fucking late after a fucking scone-related-emergency at work—note to self, do not let Abby near the oven again, even with pre-mixed dough and detailed instructions—I would insist on fucking Gigi up against the wall by my front door in that fucking fantastic dress.

"Fuck," I groan as she lifts the hem of the slinky, emerald-green number, revealing sheer black stockings and satiny garters.

Garter belts.

"Fuck, fuck, holy fuck," I mutter again.

She laughs as she lets the dress drop back into place around her legs. "You say fuck a lot when you're stressed."

"I'm not stressed." I run a hand over my rumpled, kitchen-scented hair. "I'm hard. And it's your fault."

"It's your fault for asking to see my stockings. And if you're not stressed, you should be." She glances at the delicate gold watch on her wrist. "You have exactly seventy minutes to shower and get your sexy ass to the venue. And traffic is awful heading to Williamsburg at rush hour on Fridays."

"I'll take the tube," I say offhandedly, earning myself a frustrated sigh from my oh-so-sexy partner in crime.

Ah, *partner*.

I like the thought a little more every time it drifts through my head.

"No, West," she says patiently, "I told you, there's no easy way to get there from here on the subway. You'd either have to go all the way into Manhattan first or transfer twice in Brooklyn and then catch a bus and you'll—"

"Never get there on time," I finish just as a car horn honks outside. I shoo her off. "Go. Get settled. I'll see you there."

She hesitates, her brow furrowing. "Maybe you should just come with me in the car now. You look better with a five o'clock shadow and sticky kitchen face than most men look after an hour of primping."

"There's plenty of time for me to primp. Go."

"But I—"

"Go," I insist. "I'm a big boy, I can take care of myself and *you* later tonight, after I win and you do a striptease for me to celebrate."

She rolls her eyes. "Silly, man, I'm doing a striptease for you no matter who wins." Then she winks, blows me a kiss, and hurries out the door to the car.

I watch her through the glass beside the door for a moment.

She looks damn good walking away from me. And even better headed back the other direction.

Making a mental note to ask her to move in with me as soon as it's remotely appropriate—two more weeks? Maybe one? Or tonight?— I take the stairs two at a time and rush through a shower.

* * *

Seventy-five minutes later, I'm stuck in traffic at least ten minutes from the venue—a hotel in Williamsburg with a large rooftop beer garden where we'll be cooking as the sun sets.

But it's fine. It's not like I need a tour of my station this time around. I know the ropes, and I'll be there long before the actual cooking starts.

Still, I pull out my cell and text Gigi.

West: In the car. Going to be a few minutes late, but almost there.

She texts back quickly.

Gigi: Oh good. I want you to check your station very carefully when you get here. Hawley's looking far too pleased with himself.

Grimacing, I reply.

West: Abby isn't there, is she? She said she might swing by if things weren't too crowed at the shop tonight. If she does, and Hawley says something awful to her, or so much as looks at her the wrong way, I might really have to punch him.

Gigi sends over an angry face emoji, then an explanation.

Gigi: I'll hold his arms for you, but no. She's not here. But I think she'll be fine if she does show. The fling with the hot bus boy has been good for her self-esteem.

My eyes bulge.

West: What? She's banging the hot busboy? You mean Eduardo? When did this happen?

My phone rings and I answer it to hear Gigi whisper softly, "Yes, Eduardo. Don't pretend you don't know which one is the hot busboy. And it's been happening for a little over a week and she's having amazing orgasms and he's very generous and complimentary and makes her feel beautiful and everything is fine. But now you have to pretend I didn't tell you. I thought you already knew, or I wouldn't have said a word. I don't share girl talk with people outside the girl-talk bubble, not even you."

"He's barely old enough to drink," I grunt.

"And she's still in her twenties, and it's fine, and you can relax about that. But not about Hawley." She makes a gagging sound. "Ugh. He's giving off super oily vibes tonight, like the cat who pooped in the cocoa. Get here and go over everything in your area with a fine-tooth comb."

I promise I will, whisper a few PG-rated things about how eager I am to see her in that dress again—my driver doesn't seem to be listening, but it's hard to tell—and end the call.

At the hotel, I bound out of the car and into the lobby, where I'm met by a frizzy-haired woman with kind brown eyes. "I'll show you up. I'm with the contest organizers."

We take the express elevator to the roof and step out into a sun-drenched fairyland.

This beer garden is truly a *garden*, filled with planters overflowing with flowers, potted hedges that form natural dividers between the seating areas, and even a few trees that seem to be growing straight out of the roof in the center of the space. The cooking stations are at the opposite end of the open area. Since there isn't a tent this time, I easily spot Gigi standing next to Mr. Skips.

Her hair catches the sunset and glows a brilliant ruby red. The light shimmers on her dress too, making it look like she's glittering all over, like a 1950's movie star lit to her best advantage, destined to break a million hearts.

But not mine.

I know, as soon as she sees me, that bombshell smile of hers will make me feel like I'm the only man in the room. Or on the roof.

My lips are already curving up at the edges, but when I reach the pantry staging area where the other contestants are selecting their staple ingredients for tonight's Death by Chocolate challenge, Gigi doesn't turn my way.

And she doesn't smile.

In fact, she looks like she's about to be sick. She tips her head down, shoulders curling. She nods at something Mr. Skips is saying and presses two fingers between her eyebrows.

"What's going on?" I ask Willow softly once I make my way to where she's busy by the flour canisters. I nod toward Gigi and Mr. Skips, but she clearly already knows what I'm talking about.

She shakes her head. "I don't know. Mr. Skips said he had to talk to Gigi and pulled her aside a few minutes ago. He looked really upset."

"So does she," I murmur.

"She should," an oily voice announces behind me. It's Hawley, of course, sticking his nose where it isn't wanted. I turn to glare at him—eye to eye—and then turn back around without another word.

Unfortunately, the Cut Direct doesn't work this time.

"Clearly, she thought she could get away with it," he continues. "But cheaters always get theirs, sooner or later."

I whirl back around. "Yes, they do. Is now a good time for yours?" I lift my fists. "I've got one for cheating on my sister like the sad, pitiful prick you are, and another for whatever you did to Gigi."

"I didn't do anything," Hawley says, but he takes a step back. "Aside from a little digging on your girl-friend. And I didn't have to dig very deep. She didn't even try to cover her tracks. There's a picture of her with Mr. Skips right on the community page of her website." His eyes glitter with ugly satisfaction. "She's holding his hand by a giant pie her mother made for some street fair twenty years ago."

I scowl. "What the hell are you talking about?"

"He's talking about the fact that I've known Mr. Skips since I was a kid," Gigi's says from my right, her voice tight with choked-back tears.

I shift my gaze, my chest filling with knives as I see the tragic, shame-filled look on her face.

"The organizers aren't allowed to choose family or close friends as contestants," she continues. "Mr. Skips didn't think we'd spent enough time together for me to be out of the running, but once someone pointed out how long we've known each other..." She shoots a cutting look Hawley's way. "Well, the other organizers agreed that I should be disqualified." She swallows and says to the group at large. "So... I'm out. I won't be competing tonight."

I go cold, my heart frozen.

This can't be happening to my Gigi.

I have to do something.

Some of the contestants murmur dismayed, sincere-sounding apologies, but Hawley just stands there, smugly beaming.

Gloating.

So bloody pleased with himself for ruining an innocent woman's dream, for snatching her one shot at something that matters right out from under her.

I won't let him get away with it.

No Cut Direct this time.

I've got another plan.

One that'll make all my feelings absolutely clear.

In seconds, I have the flour canister in my hands and upended over Hawley, raining wheat flour all over his wretched head.

Oh, well. Who uses wheat flour with chocolate anyway?

He sputters and lets out a shocked, squawking sound. His arms fly out to the sides, and his shoulders hunch as flour slides down the back of his flamingo print button-down shirt to stain the back of his navy pants.

"You miserable fucking wanker," he finally sputters out. "But thanks. Now you'll be disqualified too."

"But it was an accident," Willow pipes up from beside me, steel in her voice I haven't heard before. "Wasn't it, everyone?"

"Yeah, just flew off the shelf," the young guy in the purple apron says.

"Must have been the wind," adds the older woman who specializes in flan as the rest of the assembled crew make noises of agreement.

Clearly no love lost for Hawley here.

"You'd better get to your station," Willow adds in a soft yet slightly ominous voice. "Before something else accidentally falls on you." Then she pelts him with one of the chocolate chips from the cup in her hand.

It hits him in the neck and lodges in a mound of flour near his collar.

Hands curling into fists, he storms away with a huff.

After he's gone, I realize he's not the only one who's made a run for it.

I search every inch of the rooftop, but Gigi's vanished.

Gone. Like she was never here to start with.

27

GIGI

I thought I knew embarrassment when I vomited all over Christy Cannon's bathroom door during her eighth-grade Christmas party. I'd drunk eggnog, like a fool. I'd wanted to see if I was still allergic to eggs.

The verdict?

Disgustingly, violently allergic.

Half my class saw me yak up a yule log before I could make it to the toilet.

That felt like a ten on the one-to-ten scale of life's most horrifying moments.

Then, there was Theodore, watching me slide with a look that said I couldn't be more horrifically uncool or embarrassing if I tried.

Those moments feel tiny compared to this one.

As the elevator doors open, releasing me into the lobby, I want to race out of here, tear down the street, leave this all behind.

But I hate running, and I'm wearing two-inch pumps.

My heart thrashes inside my chest, mortified by what I've done.

Fine, what I did wasn't *technically* awful.

But the fact that I messed up so publicly, in front of everyone I respect, Hawley aside, *is* awful.

The fact that West and Willow and Mr. Skips and the other contest organizers and everyone I wanted to impress saw me step in it makes me feel so very small.

And it's my fault.

I didn't pay close enough attention to the rules.

I missed the caveat. The catch.

And now I just served up my aching, tender heart on a platter for everyone to feast on. *Hi, I'm Gigi, and I've been disqualified for being an idiot.*

"I should have known better," I mutter as I march out of the hotel, rustling around in my bag for my sunglasses.

I find a pair and shove them on my face, but not before fat, salty tears streak down my cheeks.

My throat tightens, a hard, hot knot of humiliation.

Yes, this is more than a ten.

My eyes sting, and I gulp back more tears. But they're relentless, determined to flood my eyes.

Outside in the muggy evening air, I make my way to the subway that'll take me home, and my phone buzzes.

Rooting around in my purse, I grab it, spying a notification. A text from West.

All my emotions try to throttle me.

Amid all the awfulness, a spark of hope flares inside. I can't help it. I want West to stay and beat the shit out of Hawley, but I also want him here with me. I want to run away with him, find somewhere safe to curl up together, and let him hold me as I drown in a sea of tears.

He's just so good at holding me, and right now I feel so small and ashamed and alone.

My heart slams against my ribs.

I hope.

I hope so damn hard.

West: Fuck, that was awful. I'm so sorry, love. Are you okay? What do you need? How can I help? Tell me, and I'll do it.

The knot in my throat tightens impossibly more, and tears slip faster down my cheeks.

Such a simple question.

So hard to answer.

But as much as the wounded part of me wants him right here, right now…

Gigi: You need to kick Hawley's ass in the contest. I'm going home. Just need to be alone for a while, but I'm fine. I swear. And I'm rooting for you! Talk later.

I add a gif.

GIF OF SASSY WOMAN SAYING GO KICK ASS

I close my phone, stuff it into my purse, and head to the subway entrance, proud of myself despite the black hole of pain in my chest.

This is my fault, and I should be alone with my misery and broken dreams. No need to drag West down with me.

Especially when I suspect he wouldn't really understand my devastation.

But I don't care if it's *just a contest*.

It wasn't just a game to me.

This was a chance to prove myself—to my community, my family, and myself. And I let it slip through my fingers by forgetting that contests have rules.

You can't just buy any property you want on Monopoly. You have to land on it. And you have to have the money.

You don't get to make up words in Scrabble.

And you don't get to enter contests you're desperate to win without studying the fine print.

"Stupid," I mutter. "Stupid girl." But as I'm about to round the corner and start down the steps to the train, I spot a taxi stopped at the light.

Unoccupied.

Rush hour has died down.

I can grab that cab and let it whisk me home without baring my mascara-streaked cheeks to dozens of strangers. Or, knowing my luck, one of my regulars will be on the train, and I'll have to explain why I'm a mess to a concerned patron who will, from this day forward, think of me as a crybaby loser.

Thrusting a hand into the air, I hail the cab with a whistle added in for good measure.

As the light changes, the yellow car jerks out of its lane and shimmies toward the curb. I jog the ten feet to the door, praying I won't tumble and crack open my chin.

Stitches would be the cherry on this shit ice cream sundae.

I grab the door handle with a rush of relief and slide into the taxi, give the driver the address, and slump down in the sticky, cracked leather seat.

Then I turn to the window, and hope grips my heart, squeezing it harder than I expect with the wish that I'll see West coming after me.

28

GIGI

There it is.

My secret, selfish wish.

To find West running after me.

Racing along the sidewalk, flagging me down. Hell, maybe he'd even dart onto the street, bang on the window as the cab pulls into traffic, and shout *stop the car.*

Then he'd grab the handle, slide inside, and gather me close. Tell me he couldn't dominate the chocolate challenge because he'd rather be with me.

Screw the damn chocolate, love. Let me smother you in kisses, instead.

Yes, I want my prince to save me.

Then I catch sight of myself in the rearview mirror and wince.

Cringe.

I look like a penguin who's been attacked by a sea otter. Those deceptively sweet-looking creatures are actually twisted creeps. No one wants to hear the ugly truth about otters.

But that's who they are.

And that's who Hawley is. He's an evil otter, and I am a wounded penguin. I don't want a magnificent unicorn man like West who always has his horn and lush coat all together to see me like this.

That would be worse than Theodore sneering from the bottom of the slide. Many times worse than running into Nelson on the street with his new girlfriend.

Thank God, the sidewalk is empty of unicorns and West *isn't* chasing me after all. He'd see the worst of me.

My flawed, hyper-critical side that hates disappointing others and really hates disappointing myself.

I've done both today, by massive amounts.

I don't want West to know how much I'm hurting right now.

He'd think I'm being ridiculous.

Someone who feels too much, who loses perspective, who's too intense about too many trivial, embarrassing things.

Most people can't handle big displays of emotion and Lord knows mine are a kitchen explosion waiting to happen. I'm a chili pot of feelings, bubbling over to scorch on the burner.

Leaving an awful, stinky mess.

What if he doesn't like this side of me? The side that occasionally loses control and ruins her makeup. The side that takes things too personally and sees every tiny failure as a sign she's fundamentally flawed.

If West saw this side of me, he'd leave. That's what

people do. They see you can't always keep your shit together, no matter how hard you try, and...they leave.

Or they simply don't show up in the first place.

My parents never showed up. And I've never had a man show up, either. I've never had a boyfriend stand by me when I stumbled, let alone fell flat on my face.

Better that West doesn't see how flat I am right now.

When I see him again, I'll be the me he loves.

The fabulous, dressy, confident me.

Not the penguin-mauled-by-an-otter me.

Only two people get to see gross, mortified Gigi. The two people who will never leave me, no matter what.

I lean forward, give the cabby a new address, then text my gram, letting her know I need pie stat.

And her.

And my brother.

With them, I'm always safe.

I try to be grateful for that, to play the gratitude game for my two fonts of unconditional love.

The people who have always been by my side, through the years.

My sun and my moon, and I love them both to the bottom of my messy, needy soul and back.

As the cabby drives, I try to convince myself I don't need—or want—more.

But I miss West terribly.

It turns out I'm not very good at gratitude tonight.

Or anything else.

29

GIGI

At Gram's, I stumble through the door and dive bomb into her couch, stuffing my face into a cushion, hiding.

"Oh, sweetie pie, what happened?" She sits next to me, petting my hair like she did when I was younger. When I'd escape to her house for comfort and a break from trying to keep my parents from breaking.

"Is this about the contest?" she presses. "You should be there now, right?"

The couch sinks near my feet. Harrison. He lives just down the block and, like Gram, he's always there when I need him. I'm so lucky, but I still feel so fucking awful. The thirty-minute cab ride did nothing to banish the misery gnawing away in my chest.

My brother squeezes my ankle. "Yeah, she should be. I was actually on my way there when you called, Gram. I was going to surprise her with this."

I look up to see Harrison holding a tiny trophy like the ones we used to win at the field day races in elementary school. Upon closer inspection, I see the plaque at the bottom reads—*Top Goddess of Pie Mountain, Bitches, And Don't You Forget It.*

See? These people are my sun and moon.

Fresh tears stream down my face at the sweet gesture and the story all spills out. I tell them about the rule violation and awful, miserable, smug Hawley and finish with, "So I'm out. Disqualified. I will not now or ever be Mrs. Sweet Stuff."

"That's bullshit," Harrison says with a scowl. "When's the last time you spent quality time with Mr. Skips? Or even his kids? We've barely seen them since they moved to Dumbo sixteen years ago."

I sit up with a hard sniff. "That's what I said, and Mr. Skips agreed. But the other organizers didn't, so I'm sweet stuff history." My breath shudders out as I pinch the bridge of my nose. "I just feel so stupid. And embarrassed. And ashamed of myself."

"For goodness' sake why?" Gram hugs me close with one arm as she gathers Joan—who's yowling by her ankles—onto her lap with the other. "You didn't do anything wrong."

"But I did. I should have realized there might be a conflict of interest. I should have been prepared just in case someone—"

"Stop it," Harrison cuts me off with a slice of his hand through the air. "We've talked about this before. No one can prepare for everything that could possibly go wrong. There is no Girl Scout with that many badges, Geeg. No superhero with that many special powers. Trust me."

I shake my head. "But I skimmed right over the fine print. Who does that?"

Gram huffs. "Everyone. For all I know, I've sold my soul to the devil a thousand times over. I haven't read a cell phone agreement or disclosure on my meds in years."

Before I can chide Gram about ignoring possible drug interactions, she continues, "And what about your new friend? How did he take the news?"

I bite my bottom lip, fighting another wave of tears. "West texted right after to ask what he could do to help. And I told him to stay and beat Hawley, and he did stay. Even though he's told me a dozen times the contest isn't a big deal to him. And now..." I flail an arm in the general direction of Williamsburg. "He's probably deep in dark chocolate soufflé mode by now. And I'm glad, I really am, but..."

"But you wanted him to come after you, which is understandable," Gram says, shushing Joan when the big floofy beast meows in irritation, clearly not happy that Gram is still rubbing me instead of her.

"But also understandable that he stayed," Harrison counters. "He knows you, right?"

I nod and sniff.

"So, he knows you're competitive as hell and winning Mrs. Sweets was important to you," he says.

I nod again.

"And you flat-out told him to stay." Harrison is in big bossy brother mode now. "And because he's a full-grown man who trusts the full-grown woman he's dating to know her own mind, he respected your wishes and stayed to fight for the both of you. Even though it isn't his top priority." With an eyebrow arch that says *you got what you asked* for, he pauses before adding in a softer voice, "And even though you aren't there to cheer him on."

I press a fist to my chest, a horrible suspicion rising inside of me. "Oh no. I should have stayed, shouldn't I? Even though I'm a gross, blubbering, mortified mess."

"No, baby," Gram says. "What you *should* do is be kinder to yourself. You should have started about thirty years ago, and I should have done a better job of helping you."

Joan takes a sneaky swipe at my skirt, claws fully bared. The cat has never scratched me outright, but she's shredded her share of innocent clothing in her attempts to show me my place.

Which is *second* place. Behind her majesty, the princess.

But Gram catches the cat's paw.

Fitting, since Gram never made me feel second best. "You did," I assure her. "That's why I'm here. Because I know I'm loved. Safe, no matter what."

"But you should be safe and loved anywhere," Gram insists. "Anywhere *you* are. Anywhere you want to be. You're always worthy of that. You don't have to be perfect all the time or do everything right. That's your birthright."

I swallow hard, rolling her words and Harrison's over in my head, mashing them together like ingredients in a pie crust.

Mixing until they come together.

Maybe I'm like a pie, one that just needed a little more time in the oven. A little more love—from these two people, but mostly from the baker.

From myself.

I'm the only one who can give me *that*.

It's my choice. I don't have to be *just so*.

I can be just me.

"If I weren't so hard on myself," I say in a halting voice as the new possibilities emerge, "then I wouldn't have been so upset. And I would have been able to stay."

And be there for West.

Be there for my man.

Harrison smiles proudly, squeezes my hand. "Or to stay even if you *were* upset, trusting that it's okay to feel the way you feel. That there's no shame in having a cry in public once and a while."

I level a hard look at my brother's always-in-control face. "When's the last time you cried in public?"

"Second grade, I think," he says with a soft laugh. He shrugs. "But I'm still a work in progress. And I'm a guy. That has its own set of challenges. I'm supposed to be strong and tough and take the lead. I bet it wasn't easy for West to stay there and let you go. I'm sure a part of him wanted to ride to the rescue, despite your wishes."

I mash that into the pie crust too, and it almost sticks, but…

"But what if he *doesn't* think it's okay to cry in public?" I whisper, a little afraid to say this next part, even in front of Gram and Harrison. They know my horrid dating history, of course, but I've never let on, even to them, how much it's messed me up. How much it's made me doubt I'm worthy of that safe, loved space Gram's talking about. "What if he's like the other men I've dated. What if the second I show weakness or a side of myself he doesn't like, he's out the door?"

"Then he's not the right man," Harrison says.

"And he's not worthy of you." Gram tucks Joan between her leg and the arm of the couch then turns to face me fully, taking my hands in her smaller ones. "And maybe West *isn't* the man for you. But sooner or later, you're going to meet someone who sees how wonderful you are, sweet girl, and who appreciates every part of you. Even the weak parts and the scared parts. He'll realize loving those parts of you is not only his job, but his honor and privilege. Just like loving those parts of him will be yours."

Harrison swipes at his cheek with the back of his hand. I look over to see his eyes shining. I free one of my hands so I can wrap an arm around him. "You okay?" I ask.

"Don't mind me," he says, the words thick. "Just kind of looking forward to that. Sounds pretty special."

"It is," Gram says, giving my hand another squeeze before she pulls away. "So is the bond between a woman and the cat who hates the entire world on her behalf. I'm going to take Joan into the kitchen for a treat before she has a meltdown and tries to assassinate the drapes. Be right back with pie and ice cream."

"Actually, I won't have time for pie." I pull in a deep breath. "I'm going back. If I hurry, maybe I can get there before they announce the winners."

"You're sure?" Gram asks. "No pressure here, either way."

I nod. "Yes, I want to be there for West, even if I am a bedraggled baby penguin."

Harrison frowns. "Excuse me?"

"Long story," I say, grabbing my bag from the floor beside the couch. "I'll tell you later." I start for the door then pause and turn back. "Or maybe I won't. I don't think you really want to know. But I will tell you this—" I point at one dear one and then the other. "I love you both. Thank you for giving it to me straight."

"Haven't given it to anyone straight since junior high," Harrison deadpans.

I wiggle my finger his way again. "Which reminds me. West's oldest brother plays for your team. So maybe, if all goes well…"

He hums beneath his breath. "I get laid by a hot Brit at your wedding?"

"I was thinking double wedding, but whatever sounds good to you," I tease, some of the old spring in my step as I wave goodbye to Gram and hurry out the door.

But on my way back to the competition, in my third car of the night, I'm nervous again.

Nervous, but determined to do my best by the man I love.

If my best isn't enough, that's okay, too. Gram and Harrison are right. I don't have to be perfect. I just have to give my full heart and be good to myself, even when I fall short.

And if I'm lucky, I'll get to be good to West too, even when he falls short.

Surely, even unicorns have an off day now and then. I just hope I get to be there for him on those days.

And all the ones between.

30

WEST

Two hours and twelve minutes.

I'd be lying if I said I wasn't aware of every second that's dragged by since Gigi left. Every moment I've spent tending a fussy dark chocolate soufflé on this rooftop while wishing I were wherever she is now.

But I had a job to do and, damn it, I did it.

I have no doubt this chocolate creation is orgasmic.

Now, it's in the judge's hands, and I hope it's enough to take home the prize.

But not for me. For Gigi. For the woman I adore, who left her parting orders—*Kick Hawley's arse.*

Mission accepted.

Now, as the sun dips toward the horizon, pulling the day away with it, I send out a wish—on my mother's memory and on the love she left me along with her soufflé recipe—that the rest of the evening will go as I hope.

Mr. Skips huddles with the judges then clears his

throat and approaches the microphone, ready to announce the winners.

He stands before the crowd in a seersucker suit and a panama hat, beaming with pride. But there's disappointment too, likely over Gigi's ousting.

I get it. I *feel* it. Justice didn't win out today, and the only way to make that even slightly more palatable is if someone other than Hawley wins the prize.

Please, let it be someone other than that fucking weasel...

Please don't let him win. Not when I'm out of flour and sugar and all other easy-to-dump-over-an-asshole's-head materials.

Though, I do a have a few leftover eggs I can toss if needed...

"Every day is better with a little sugar in it," Mr. Skips says, patting his rotund belly. "Believe me, I know." He holds for polite chuckles from the audience parked at the picnic tables scattered across the roof. "But I have no guilt about my love of sweets, cakes, chocolates, and treats. Like my grandmother, the wedding cake queen of Brooklyn, always said: *The world can always use more of two things—love and frosting.* And that's why she started this contest, to celebrate the sweet things in life. So, without further ado, I'm pleased to announce our top three contestants. In third place is —" He takes a beat to scan his index card. I clench my fists, nerves tearing through me. "Frederick James Ebenezer Hawley."

Ha! Brilliant.

Bloody fucking brilliant!

I stifle a whoop of victory as I whip my gaze to the

tosser. Hawley's doing a stellar impression of a beet, slowly turning red as embarrassment floods his neck, his face, even his beady little eyeballs.

The sore-loser scarlet matches his polo shirt perfectly as he pastes on a thin-lipped smile, giving a simpering thank you nod that makes me want to punch him. But doesn't everything?

Now I have a very real shot at the top prize.

Like Gigi wanted.

Like she hoped.

But all I can think is that she should be here.

That she would love to see this.

And then, a vision in emerald emerges from the elevator.

Is that...?

I squint as the redhead steps onto the rooftop garden with her hand raised to shield her eyes from the fading sun as she scans the line of chefs gathered in front of our stations.

It's her.

My Gigi.

She's a little messy—dress wrinkled, hair pulled into a crooked ponytail, mascara smudged beneath her eyes —but she's still beautiful.

Maybe even more beautiful.

Because I know she showed up messy and in a rush for me. So we could share this victory—or defeat —together.

But I honestly don't care anymore which it is. All I want is her.

It seems she feels the same. The moment our eyes

connect, she starts across the garden at a jog.

I jolt away from my station but stop myself before I go more than a few steps. I don't want to steal Mr. Skips's limelight.

The older man's clever eyes bounce between the two of us, and his lips stretch into a sly little smile. "Just a moment, sweet-lovers of all ages. There's a very close call here for first and second place. I'll need to confer with the judges for a moment." He trundles over to the judge's table, giving me all the opportunity I need.

I close the distance to Gigi as she rushes to me, throwing her arms around my neck and pressing a kiss to my cheek. "I need to tell you something important," she says, her words spilling out at Mach speed. "I love you. And I'd still love you if you didn't have a library, or if you lived in a tiny room in the back of Tea and Empathy and your clothes always smelled like scones. I'd love you if you didn't wear suits. I'd love you if you didn't drink fifty-year-old whiskey or have the world's greatest board game collection. Because the way I feel for you has nothing to do with any of that."

She clasps my face, stroking my jaw as she delivers the very best love speech. Better, even, than the one on the Ferris wheel. That was fantastic, but this is one for the ages.

"I love everything about you. Your witty brain and your gorgeous face and your big heart, and the way you keep things in perspective, even when it's hard," she says before adding with a soft smile, "And I love that you insist you aren't running late even when you are. And that you refuse to stress even when you probably should. And that you look down your nose at bankers, even though you used to be one, and that you are very snotty about socks."

I hug her closer. "My feet demand a certain standard of heel cushioning and reinforcement."

"I know they do," she says. "And I love that you insist on getting what you need, even when it means leaving for your morning run when I'd rather you stay in bed and snuggle." She sighs and her brows pinch together. "I just...wanted you to know. That I love you like that. And that I'm kind of hoping you might love me the same way."

Before I can insist that I adore every fucking thing about her from her poise, loyalty, intelligence, and killer sex-appeal to the way she leaves empty coffee cups all over the house and constantly misplaces her purse, Mr. Skips returns to the microphone. "All right, we're all sorted! In second place is West Byron."

I freeze, then blink.

Well...

Good.

If things pan out the way I think they have, this is actually quite good.

As if reading my mind, a wide-eyed Gigi lifts her crossed fingers between us.

"And the winner, for her absolutely incredible, sinfully delicious chocolate indulgence molten cake, is"—Mr. Skips takes a dramatic beat—"Willow Thompson."

"Oh, my." Gigi claps her hand over her mouth, clearly thrilled. Then as she joins in the applause echoing through the garden, she glances up at me. "You're not upset, are you?"

I shake my head. "Couldn't be less upset, in fact. You?"

She beams. "No. Not a bit. She totally deserves this. One hundred percent."

As soon as the clapping and cheering dies down a little, Gigi takes my hand and pulls me over to Willow, throwing her arms around the dog-loving cupcake baker. "I'm so happy for you! You're going to be an incredible Mrs. Sweets."

"Thank you. I can't quite believe it yet," Willow says in an awed voice. "I never expected I might actually win."

Gigi smiles. "I did. You're an incredible baker. And your cupcakes are the best in the city. We should celebrate! You want to get lunch tomorrow?"

"I would love to," says the once shy, still shy, but now bolder woman.

When a beaming older couple—Willow's parents I'm guessing—whisk her away for pictures with Mr. Skips, I guide Gigi to a quiet corner of the garden, gather her into my arms, and return all my attention to her. "What's come over you, woman? Where's my ruthless competitor? My Scrabble destroyer?" I ask with a laugh.

She shrugs coquettishly then leans closer, whispering just for me. "Oh, she's here. She's definitely here." Her tone turns serious, a touch emotional. "And I was really upset to be disqualified, but I didn't want to let that keep me from being present for the people I care about. Like Willow. And you. Especially you. You're so...good, West. Honestly, sometimes I think I don't deserve you."

I furrow my brow. "Nonsense. Stop that. That's not true."

She presses her hand to my chest. "No, I want to say this. I can be foolish and silly sometimes."

"Silly in a good way," I insist.

Her lips quirk. "Thanks, but silly in a bad way, too. I know that. That's just...part of who I am. Sometimes I'm going to make embarrassing mistakes or have it less together than I'd like. And I will probably never be as cool as you are."

I start to scoff again, but she continues, "I hope that's okay. I want to be open and honest with you. I just want to be...me. And for you to be you. And to know we'll forgive each other when we fall short and maybe even love each other more for it."

My heart soars. I came to New York determined to keep my dating life casual and uncomplicated. But that determination is long gone. I want complicated. I want happy and sad, rain and shine, good and bad with this woman.

"I want all of those things, with you and only with you. *Always* with you." I run my knuckles along her cheek. "And I think you're the cool one."

She huffs. "Yeah?"

"The fucking coolest." I tuck her hair behind her ear. "You're wonderful, even when you're messy."

Her smile looks like she's starting over, learning to let go. "Thank you. I'm going to do a better job of that— being okay with a little mess. I hear it makes you a better, happier person." She arches a playful brow. "Not to mention girlfriend."

I lean in and press a soft kiss to those lips I love. "You're already the best girlfriend, but I love this plan. And I love you. All of you. I didn't just fall in love with the outside, you know. I'm mad for that fierce, brave, and loyal heart of yours. And I'm going to keep it safe, Gigi. I promise."

"Good." Her breath hitches and her eyes shine. "Because it's yours, West. It's all yours."

I cup her cheeks, drawing her in close for a kiss as night falls across my adopted city.

Neither of us won the day, but as I kiss the woman I adore, I know I'm taking home the biggest prize of all.

* * *

Once we reach my place, we fall together onto the couch.

Her dress comes off. Her bra. Her knickers. My trousers. All our clothes vanish.

Then my Gigi straddles me and drops down on top of me deliciously. I fill her in one hot thrust, savoring the tightness, feeling like I've come home. I run my hands up her back, loving the soft slide of her skin. I make love to her and do all the things we like best.

I smack her arse, pull her hair, and kiss her madly. I glide a hand between her legs, touching her where she wants me most.

Like I did the first night. Like I intend to every night.

It's a gift when the woman you love shows you all

the pieces of herself, and I mean to treasure every part of Gigi.

To treasure *her*.

To give her love and a ridiculous number of orgasms.

After number five or six, I take her hand, clasping it as I catch my breath with my cock still buried inside her. "You are my favorite thing about New York. Aside from that T-shirt we won on our first date, of course."

She nods seriously. "Understandable. That's a sweet shirt."

"Not as sweet as you are." I kiss her neck and murmur against her warm skin, "Is it okay that I can't get enough of you?"

"No," she teases. "I demand to be sent home right away. No more orgasms, no strip Scrabble in the library, no champagne in the claw-foot tub."

I pull back to gaze down at her with a wicked grin. "I'm going to destroy you at strip Scrabble."

"Not if I destroy you first," she says, her eyes glittering.

"You're a very bad woman. You know that?"

She cups my face. "How can I help it, when you make it feel so good? Now, get dressed and take me to your library, you sexy beast, and let's see how fast I can get you naked again."

We do just that.

And it's very bad.

And oh-so-good.

And something I hope lasts for a very long time, indeed.

31

GIGI

Four months later...

"No. I refuse to cave under your interrogation tactics!" Abby crosses her arms and sits on the wooden stool in the corner of the courtyard behind Tea and Empathy, shivering in the evening breeze. "West will have my head if I tell you anything except that he'll be here by seven."

"No, he won't," I say. "He'll have your head if he finds out you and Eduardo are still having sex in the basement before he gets here every morning."

Her eyes go wide. "You wouldn't."

"Of course I wouldn't." I bat my lashes. "As long as you tell me what West was up to this morning."

"Gigi, seriously. What else am I supposed to do with those twenty minutes?" she deflects. "Sit around and watch the scones bake when there's a perfectly beautiful man just waiting for me to fly down the stairs and jump on him like a primal tigress? Don't you agree I have a duty to embrace my inner tigress?"

I fight a grin. One thing I've learned about Abby in the past few months—she'll say anything for a laugh, and if you let her know she's getting to you, she'll never stop.

It's amazing to see her blossom post-Hawley. Even more amazing to see Hawley's frozen food empire begin to crumble after he was sued by three former girl-friends, all alleging he stole not only their recipes, but several family heirlooms.

But seriously, right now this woman needs to give me the goods before I perish from curiosity. "Of course, I believe in honoring the primal tigress," I say, "but West is more concerned with health code violations."

"Ugh. You're so right. He's such a stick in the mud like that." She narrows her eyes. "Though, if *you* were waiting for *him* in the basement, you can bet your sweet ass he'd be violating the health code—and you—ten different ways."

"Or twenty," I agree.

"See, total double standard." Then she thinks for a moment, her brow furrowing, and adds, "Really? Twenty? I can't think of that many positions off the cuff. You two really are a pair of perverts, aren't you?"

"Very much so. Perverts who promised to get kinky together over a few spreadsheets this morning before a conference call with Willow about our cross-promo-tional flavor selections for December. But instead, your brother cancelled at the last minute, ran out the door like a madman, and has been very cagey about his whereabouts all day."

Abby raises her eyes to study the darkening sky. "But that's going so well, right? The cross-promo customer loyalty thing? The businesses are all growing. Profits are growing. Customers are happy. It's brilliant, really."

"Mr. Skips is brilliant. And you keep changing the subject."

She sighs. "Well, it's something I'm good at, I confess. When you grow up the youngest of four siblings, the only girl, and weirdly small, you learn pretty quickly that disarming your opponent with words is your only path to victory." Glancing over my shoulder, she spots something that makes her slump with relief. "Speaking of victory, I won this bet, West." Abby hops off her stool. "You owe me fifty bucks."

I turn to see him crossing the cobblestones in his navy three-piece suit, and my heart flips the way it always does. I assumed all the flipping would calm down eventually, but if anything, it seems to be getting worse.

One look at this man—*my* man—and I'm as giddy as the night I first brought him home.

"Really? You didn't cave and confess?" he asks her as he wraps an arm around my waist.

"No, she didn't." I lean into him, accepting the kiss he presses to my cheek. "But you'd better start talking. You know I hate surprises."

He and Abby both laugh. *Hard.*

"What?" I frown and amend. "Okay, so I love surprises, but not surprises that take you away from me on our day off."

Abby hums beneath her breath as she starts across the courtyard. "Oh, you're going to like this one." She pauses in the door leading into the shop. "See you two at Ruby's gallery later for the opening?"

"See you there," West assures her, adding under his breath as she leaves, "Though, I don't see how we're all going to fit. The place is the size of a postage stamp."

I grin. "But a cute postage stamp. And she's so excited about this series. She's done portraits of all her favorite Brooklyn restaurant owners as animals. The ones I've seen so far are precious. And all proceeds are going to the local food pantry, so..."

"We're obligated to buy at least twelve pieces?"

"I was thinking two." I arch a brow. "But you do have that entire empty wall by the refrigerator. Pictures of foodie animals would liven things up over there."

"Agreed." He shoots me one of his fond smiles that makes me feel completely adored and so very lucky.

I know I make him feel the same way, and I'd love to indulge him by being super patient, but... "I really can't wait," I whisper as he takes my hand. "I need to know what you were up to before it literally kills me."

"Literally kills?" he echoes, leading me into the empty shop. "Are you sure about that?"

After realizing almost all their business happens before three, Tea and Empathy started closing at three on weekdays and four on weekends. Meanwhile, I hired additional staff to take the shipping arm of the business off my hands and free up my nights for things more fun than bookkeeping and website maintenance. Work smarter, not harder, is our new motto, and we're both reaping the rewards in more profitable sweet shops and more time together after work.

"Yes, literal death," I insist, pressing a hand to my ribs with a wince. "I can feel it now. Need to Know is stabbing my spleen."

"And once you lose the spleen, you're really screwed."

"So screwed," I murmur.

He turns to face me beside the gourd display by the hostess's stand. "All right, then. Might as well have at it."

I blink, then narrow my eyes. "Have at what?"

"Your gift. I originally planned to surprise you in the library later, then I realized you'd be rabid with curiosity by this point, so I brought it with me."

"Oh, yay," I squeak, clapping my hands. "Thank you. I really am rabid."

He laughs. "I know." He nods toward the stand. "Pop the top."

I reach out, lifting the wooden top to expose the storage area beneath. Inside is...

My jaw drops, and I shift wide eyes West's way. "An antique Scrabble set?"

"Even better," he says proudly. "A hand-carved special edition commissioned by my great-grandfather in 1948. Here all the way from my family's estate in Canterbury."

"Oh, so pretty." I reverently lift the heavy, gorgeously carved box from the stand and set it on the table behind me.

"My father sent it over with a business friend of his. That's where I was—treating the friend to lunch as a thank you for playing messenger. He had a change to his schedule and needs to leave New York earlier than expected so…" He pulls in a breath and lets it out long and slow. "It was now or never."

I glance up with a grin. "You sound nervous. I promise I won't break it." I run a gentle hand over the wood.

"I know you won't," he whispers. "Go ahead. Open it. The suspense is killing me. I want to see if the tiles are as fancy as I remember."

"Fancy tiles, huh?" I grip the edges of the hinged case and lift. "That will make beating you even more…"

I trail off. There, on top of the closed game board, those fancy tiles spell out one word—*Always?*

I jerk my gaze back to West and say perhaps the dumbest thing ever, "This set has punctuation?"

He exhales and nods. "Yeah. I'm not sure the carver really understood the game all that well. But it adds another dimension. And is helpful at times like these." He pulls a small box from his pocket and my heart ping-pongs again as he opens it to reveal an astonishingly large diamond.

Holy. Smokes.

"This is the real reason for the hand delivery. My father wasn't about to send this via post."

I cover my mouth with my hand as tears fill my eyes, a part of me unable to believe this is happening.

"It was my great grandmother's," he says softly. "Then my mother's. And now, I'd really love for it to be yours and for you to be mine. For always."

Tears streaming down my cheeks, I hurl myself at him, wrapping my arms tight around his neck as I say, "Yes. Oh, yes. And you'll be mine, and I'm never ever going to let you go."

"I certainly hope not," he says, hugging me tight as he sighs. "I confess I'm glad that's over. I was nervous."

I pull back, grinning up at him. "You seriously thought I'd say no?"

"I thought you might think we should wait. But I couldn't put it off. I needed to see my ring on your finger. It's become an almost primal thing."

I laugh as I hold out my trembling hand. "Abby was just talking about her primal tigress. You're a very primal pair."

"Oh, God, don't tell me. If I hear any more about her sex life, I'll never be able to look poor Eduardo in the eye again." He slides the ring into place on my finger. "There we go. Beautiful."

I blink faster. "And a perfect fit."

"I had it sized. That's what else I was up to this afternoon."

"Clever man." I hold out my hand, cocking my head as I watch the diamond glint in the light. "Wow. There's only one thing that could make this moment any better."

"Sex in the basement before we go to the gallery opening?"

"I was thinking the bathroom, but…"

I race for the stairs, giggling. He follows me, and we prove that my ring looks gorgeous when my hands are braced against the brick wall while he fucks me from behind.

And then we get dressed and head to Ruby's gallery to share the good news with the people we love, and finally head home with four new paintings of our very own and a December wedding to plan.

Because we can't wait for spring or summer.

"We can stay on in London after the ballroom dancing competition," West says. "Get married in a frigid old church with no central heat, have a huge party after at my brother's fancy penthouse in Notting Hill, and then stay on for Christmas in the country with my dad and his new girlfriend."

I clap my hands. "I'll buy plane tickets for Harrison and Gram tomorrow. And Ruby and Jesse too, if they can get away."

He nods, grinning. "Abby's already going home for the holiday, so she'll be there. And the rest of my family lives in or near London, so they should be able to make it on short notice."

I brush invisible dirt from my hands. "Done. How easy was that?"

He pulls me close and kisses me deep and sweet. "So easy. Almost as easy as getting you into the sack."

I laugh against his lips. "What can I say? When it comes to you, I just can't say no, mister."

"A fact I am grateful for every day," he murmurs.

And then he proves it, confirming he's the best boyfriend—and soon to be husband—ever.

Really. Ever.

I'm not competitive about many things these days, but of this I'm quite certain. West is the very best, and I can't wait to promise him my always and forever.

EPILOGUE

Later

Joan the cat

Cats are good at a great many things— Looking fantastic literally all the time. Lazing in the sun. And sussing out people's true natures.

I excel at all of the above. I take impeccable care of my coat, I bask in the windows on bright, clear days, and I know exactly who is worthy of my love.

The woman who cares for me, of course.

Her devotion is unparalleled, and I make it my business to purr for her at least once a day. Twice, if she's exceptionally attentive.

I confess, however, that I have a suspicious heart. I tend to think the worst of humans until they prove themselves.

Lately, however…

Well, the red-haired woman who also likes to be petted by my person is growing on me. She and her mate with the funny accent, both. Red finally seems to have grasped that cats don't always want to be touched.

Perhaps her mate taught her…

I brush up against him now, treating him to a rub of my haunches against his legs, which he acknowledges with a respectful, "Thank you, gorgeous," without reaching so much as a finger in my direction.

Yes, he's a good one.

I also rather like my person's other friend. The young man with the finely brushed fur on his head. He looks at me with a pleasing mix of wariness and admiration that, frankly, all humans would do well to emulate.

He seems happier these days.

Like today.

As my person spreads cards on the table, her young man friend pulls out a chair for a new man. "Pierce, welcome to the James family tradition. Poker Sundays with Gram."

The new man chuckles. "I've been looking forward to this, Harrison. The only thing better than meeting, dating, and falling in love with an exceptionally witty and good-looking book editor was learning he has a card shark for a gram."

"We'll see if you still think that way after I take all your chips," my person teases.

The entire table laughs and sets to playing and eating obscene amounts of pie.

But, this time, Red brought me a small, chicken liver pie of my own to devour, so I'm not jealous of their treats.

I am, in fact, feeling very well-fed, pampered, and ready for a nap in the sun. I might even reward Red with a rub against her legs on my way to the window.

Then my person demands, "Since when have you refused a second cup of coffee, Gigi James? What's up your sleeve this morning? You look like the cat who got the cream."

I glance up at Red with a sniff. She looks nothing like a cat of any sort; her fur is far too wild and out of order. But I catch her exchanging glances with her mate.

"Tell them," he says. "We won't be able to keep it a secret much longer anyway. Not with two of them in there."

"Two of them." My person presses a hand to her chest as she gasps in delight. "You don't mean…"

"We're pregnant," Red says, beaming at the humans around the table. "Twins."

The gathering erupts into raucous cries and cheers.

I take advantage of the commotion to jump onto the china cabinet and settle in for a nap while my person is too distracted to fret that I'll break one of her fancy vases.

As they continue to celebrate, I drift off with a satisfied sigh, knowing I'll wake in my person's arms—she always gathers me up for a cuddle after she finds me sleeping where she thinks I shouldn't.

I look forward to it.

And to a few pieces of her leftover pie crust.

Yes, it's a good day to be a cat.

Much like every other.

* * *

Thank you for reading Gigi and West's love story! You can find the other standalone romances in the Good Love series everywhere!

ALSO BY LAUREN BLAKELY

FULL PACKAGE, the #1 New York Times Bestselling romantic comedy!

BIG ROCK, the hit New York Times Bestselling standalone romantic comedy!

THE SEXY ONE, a New York Times Bestselling standalone romance!

THE KNOCKED UP PLAN, a multi-week USA Today and Amazon Charts Bestselling standalone romance!

MOST VALUABLE PLAYBOY, a sexy multi-week USA Today Bestselling sports romance! And its companion sports romance, MOST LIKELY TO SCORE!

WANDERLUST, a USA Today Bestselling contemporary romance!

COME AS YOU ARE, a Wall Street Journal and multi-week USA Today Bestselling contemporary romance!

PART-TIME LOVER, a multi-week USA Today Bestselling contemporary romance!

UNBREAK MY HEART, an emotional second chance USA Today Bestselling contemporary romance!

BEST LAID PLANS, a sexy friends-to-lovers USA Today

Bestselling romance!

The Heartbreakers! The USA Today and WSJ Bestselling rock star series of standalone!

P.S. IT'S ALWAYS BEEN YOU, a sweeping, second chance romance!

ALSO BY LILI VALENTE

Hot Royal Romance

The Playboy Prince

The Grumpy Prince

The Bossy Prince

Learn more here

Laugh-out-Loud Rocker Rom Coms

The Bangover

Bang Theory

Banging The Enemy

The Rock Star's Baby Bargain

Learn more here

The Bliss River Small Town Series

Falling for the Fling

Falling for the Ex

Falling for the Bad Boy

Learn more here

The Hunter Brothers

The Baby Maker

The Troublemaker

The Heartbreaker

The Panty Melter

Click here to learn more

The Bad Motherpuckers Series

Hot as Puck

Sexy Motherpucker

Puck-Aholic

Puck me Baby

Pucked Up Love

Puck Buddies

Click here to learn more

Sexy Flirty Dirty Romantic Comedies

Magnificent Bastard

Spectacular Rascal

Incredible You

Meant for You

Click here to learn more

To the Bone Series

(Sexy Romantic Suspense, must be read in order)

A Love so Dangerous

A Love so Deadly

A Love so Deep

Click here to learn more

The Rebel Hearts Series

(Emotional New Adult Romantic Suspense.

Must be read in order.)

Rebel Hearts

Savage Hearts

Lover's Leap Series

A Naughty Little Christmas

The Bad Boy's Temptation

Click here to learn more

The Lonesome Point Series

(Sexy Cowboys)

Leather and Lace

Saddles and Sin

Diamonds and Dust

12 Dates of Christmas

Glitter and Grit

Sunny with a Chance of True Love

Chaps and Chance

Ropes and Revenge

8 Second Angel

Click here to learn more

Co-written Standalones

The V Card (co-written with Lauren Blakely)

Good With His Hands (co-written with Lauren Blakely)

Good To Be Bad (co-written with Lauren Blakely)

Falling for the Boss (co-written with Sylvia Pierce)

Click here to learn more

The Happy Cat Series

(co-written with Pippa Grant)

Hosed

Hammered

Hitched

Humbugged

Click here to learn more

CONTACT

We love hearing from readers! You can find Lauren on Twitter at LaurenBlakely3, Instagram at LaurenBlakely-Books, Facebook at LaurenBlakelyBooks, or online at LaurenBlakely.com. You can also email Lauren at laurenblakelybooks@gmail.com

Find Lili on Twitter at lili_valente_ro, Facebook at AuthorLiliValente, or online at LiliValente.com. You can also email Lili at lili.valente.romance@gmail.com

Printed in Great Britain
by Amazon